DEAR DAD

LAURA BEST

NIMBUS
PUBLISHING
— NIMBUS.CA —

Nimbus Publishing Limited
3660 Strawberry Hill Street, Halifax, NS, B3K 5A9
(902) 455-4286 nimbus.ca

This story is a work of fiction. Names, characters, incidents, and places, including organizations and institutions, are used fictitiously.

Printed and bound in Canada

NB1674

Editor: Penelope Jackson
Editor for the press: Claire Bennet
Design: Jenn Embree

Nimbus Publishing is based in Kjipuktuk, Mi'kma'ki, the traditional territory of the Mi'kmaq People.

Library and Archives Canada Cataloguing in Publication

Title: Dear Dad / Laura Best.
Names: Best, Laura (Laura A.), author.
Identifiers: Canadiana (print) 2024040095X | Canadiana (ebook) 20240400968 | ISBN 9781774713389 (softcover) | ISBN 9781774713396 (EPUB)
Subjects: LCGFT: Novels.
Classification: LCC PS8603.E777 D43 2024 | DDC jC813/.6—dc23

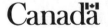  

Nimbus Publishing acknowledges the financial support for its publishing activities from the Government of Canada, the Canada Council for the Arts, and from the Province of Nova Scotia. We are pleased to work in partnership with the Province of Nova Scotia to develop and promote our creative industries for the benefit of all Nova Scotians.

In memory of my dad, John Legge

CHAPTER 1

"SIDNEY CROSBY'S THE BEST," SAYS NOAH WITH THAT glazed-over look he gets when he's watching something cool. That usually means there are zombies on the screen, except Sidney Crosby beats out zombies any day. Noah bites into a Pizza Pocket, leaving behind a string of cheese on his lip. He's waiting for Sidney to empty the bucket of water and ice over his own head. One. Two. Three. It's over in one big gush. Wouldn't want to be Sidney right now. Bet that water was colder than a polar bear's butt.

We've seen the video a hundred times and it never gets old, but then nothing about Sidney Crosby can ever get old. Noah reaches for his drink without taking his eyes off the screen. A mouthful of soda goes down with a big gulp and he lets out a huge burp. The word *manners* isn't in his vocabulary. In fact, he can belch with the best of them. I click on the next video and start watching Pascal Dupuis and his family take up the challenge. We've got it all memorized—the videos with our favourite players, that is. The Ice Bucket Challenge is sweeping through the NHL and we can't get enough of it— watching the momentum grow is awesome. People are finally becoming aware of ALS. There's been over a million bucks raised in less than two weeks.

Way to get the word out, guys. No wonder they're my heroes.

We go through the videos one last time before I shut down the computer and start gathering up our dirty dishes. I'm not a neat freak or anything. Normally I'd leave them for Mom, but she's got enough to do these days.

"We could do that, you know," says Noah, looking up at me. He's sitting in the middle of the bed, cross-legged.

I brush his stray crumbs off the comforter. Dad used to joke that a family of mice could live off the fat of the land in my room. "A smorgasbord of crumbs and leftovers," he'd laugh.

"What are you talking about?" I ask. "Do what?"

"You know—the challenge," says Noah, looking up from the bed.

"The challenge?" My head tilts to the side and I look at him, unimpressed. He's got to be kidding.

"Seriously."

"Yeah, right." I grin and grab a balled-up piece of paper towel he left behind on the bed.

"No. Listen. It's doable." By this time, his eyes are blazing and the wheels are turning fast. He scrambles to the other side of the bed and jumps to his feet. I look at him like he's nuts and turn toward the door, my hands full of dishes.

"Your dad has ALS. Don't you want to help raise money?" he says, suddenly. I stop as if I've been punched in the gut. I consider it for maybe a second, but then flick it off. It's a bad idea.

He looks over at my dresser and casually picks up the small square box that has Rosie's name engraved on it.

"What do think you're doing?" I set the dishes down on the bed. "Give me that," I say, pulling the box from his hands and putting it back. He knows I don't like anyone touching my dog. I gather up the dishes again.

"Get real," I tell him. "Like anyone's going to watch a video we make. We're not NHL stars. We're fourteen-year-old nobodies. Now get out of my way."

Noah might be my best friend, but he's always been an attention seeker. The Ice Bucket Challenge is about raising money for ALS. Who would care about us or even watch the video we made, let alone donate? We'd freeze our butts off for nothing.

"Hear me out," he says, throwing his hands in the air.

He's getting another one of his big ideas, just like the time he decided we should skip school and go to the skate park. We were twelve and didn't know what we were doing, of course we got caught. Noah couldn't keep his mouth shut. Half the school knew where we were. Lucky I didn't get grounded for life.

I stop in front of Noah; my hands are full. "Open up, dude. You're blocking my way." Some people can anticipate what needs to be done, but not Noah. Strange, because out on the ice it's totally different. Things just flow between us.

I can tell he's not going to budge until I hear what his big idea is.

"Okay. Shoot," I say.

His brown eyes light up. He's full of energy. "We can do it in front of the school!"

"School's out for the summer, genius."

"So? It's a place people will recognize right away. Better than your backyard. And I'll get the word out. Don't worry about that. I'll record it with my phone and upload it to YouTube."

"*You'll* record it?" Of course *he'll* record it. I'll be the one dumping ice water over my head. No worries about Noah taking *that* privilege away from me.

"Leave it to me. You'll see." He slaps me on the shoulder and reaches for the doorknob. No sense arguing anymore. It's all settled, at least in Noah's mind.

———

"I'll make sure to get your good side," says Noah, walking along. He's got everything all figured out. I'm the one carrying the bucket of ice down the sidewalk—the jug of water too. Good thing the school is only a few blocks away. Noah's going through the steps of what we'll do once we get there. As predicted, I'll be the one dumping the ice water over my head. I guess it's only right, since we're doing this because of Dad, but still. Might have been nice if he'd have offered.

Noah continues to go over his plans to get our video some attention on social media. All the places he's going to share it. I'm still wondering who, if anyone, is going to care. He ends with "Remember—say who you are and that you're doing this for your dad."

I know it's about ALS and us doing this for Dad. I mean, give me some credit.

I finally agreed that it makes sense to film our video out in front of Forest Glenn. Hopefully, it'll draw some attention to what we're doing if we pick a central location. Noah put the word out on social media about what's going on today. He even got in touch with the principal and set up a GoFundMe page in the school's name—so it's all legit. The rest is up to me.

When we round the corner, I stop short. There's a crowd spread out in front of the school. "What's going on?" I say, setting my things down. I look over at Noah.

"I thought it would be better if I rounded up a few people to help out."

"For real?" I look through the crowd standing in front of the school. They've all got buckets. Principal Feener is here and a ton of people I don't really know. They shout out a greeting and I wave. Unbelievable.

I look over at Noah. He's smiling like a goof. He punches me in the arm. "Come on," he says, and we hurry to join the others.

"Hope you don't mind sharing the limelight," says Mr. Feener, stepping toward us. He's decked out in khaki shorts and a white golf shirt and grinning from ear to ear. I look past him, at everyone there. They did all this for my dad. The tightness in my throat makes it hard to swallow.

"Not at all," I say. I can't believe it—none of it. Noah's not one for keeping his mouth shut. That in itself is nearing miracle status. How did he manage all this without me finding out?

Noah lets out a shrill whistle to get everyone's attention. When they're all relatively quiet, he tells us to get into position. We pour the water into our buckets of ice.

"Okay, everyone. Sam's going to set things up first and then he'll put the challenge out to Forest Glenn and two other schools in the area. Then it'll be our turn." Noah's good at giving orders.

I stand off to one side. The rest of the group is to my right. Noah gives the okay and starts recording.

"Hi, I'm Sam Gillis and I'm doing the Ice Bucket Challenge in honour of my dad, who has ALS. I'm putting the challenge out to Forest Glenn, Clayton Park, and Halifax Central." I pick up the bucket of ice water, careful not to hesitate. Making yourself look weak for the world to see is unforgiveable.

The ice water is like shards of glass hitting my skin. I want to yell, but only for a few seconds. It's got to be twenty-seven degrees Celsius outside today. I shake out my arms and legs. Noah stops recording, hurries toward me, and leans in for a fist bump. People cheer.

Next, Noah directs everyone to get ready. He steps back so he can get them all in the frame, then gives Feener his phone along with some quick instructions. He challenges three different schools in Nova Scotia. He counts to three. Everyone grabs their ice bucket. And then all I see is the icy water splashing down over Noah's coal black hair. People are gasping. The girls scream. Some of the guys play it cool, others outright yelp. Arms are flailing. The expression on Noah's face is the best. Feener catches it all on video. It's epic. I look over at Noah and do a fist pump into the air. I can't believe he went to all this trouble. We might actually raise some money.

———

I'm still feeling euphoric as we make our way home, the empty bucket swinging in my hand. I keep looking over at Noah. He's giddy too. We stop laughing and I finally get a grip.

"Can't believe you pulled this off and I didn't have a clue," I say. I cough awkwardly and add, "Thanks, man."

"No problem," he says, slapping me on the back. I know we won't break any records raising money, but we'll be able to donate a respectable amount, and that feels good. At the moment, I don't think anything could make me happier.

We walk back to my place, polish off a bag of Oreos and a half jug of milk in the kitchen. Life is good, at least for now.

———

Mom and Dad get choked up when they see the video we made. I tell them how the school joined in to raise money for ALS and that sends happy tears running down Mom's face. A few days later, a reporter from the local paper comes to take photos and interview me and Noah. For like fifteen minutes we're celebrities. But really, it's about the donations, not us, so it's fine.

"How does it feel to know your son helped raise money for ALS?" the reporter asks Mom and Dad.

"We're very proud of Sam," says Dad. There's been a big change in his speech just this past while. It kills me hearing him struggle to get the words out.

"Sam has always been a doer," Mom says to the reporter. "He gets that from his father." She looks down at Dad. Her eyes well up with tears. She pulls herself together and places her hands on Noah's shoulders. "And this one here set everything into motion. Didn't he, Sam?"

I smile. "That's right. I just dumped the ice water over my head. Noah came up with the idea and then made it happen." I'm glad Mom mentioned Noah's part in all of it. He deserves the credit.

Overnight the donations soar. In a few days, we've passed the $20,000 mark. It's mind-blowing.

"Awesome," says Noah, checking the donation page once more.

"Hey, look. It's cool that you pulled this off." I should have had faith. I shouldn't have shot down his idea at first.

"We make a great team, on and off the ice," he says. Smiling, he searches online for highlights from the latest Penguins game. He's glued to the screen, waiting for Sidney to score. I can't help thinking how hard it's going to be breaking the news to him.

CHAPTER 2

SEPTEMBER'S HERE AND IT'S A WEEK BEFORE FALL tryouts. I've got to have a serious talk with Mom and Dad but I'm not sure how to start. I'm not looking forward to this conversation, but it's better to get it over with.

Mom fusses over Dad through dinner. His food is pureed so he can swallow it easily, and she goes slowly. She's got a good system worked out: a spoonful for Dad, a few highlights about her day, a few bites from her own plate. By that time, Dad's ready for more and it starts all over again. I'm not sure if it's a conscious thing on her part or a pattern she's fallen into over time.

"Tryouts are coming up next week," I say, glancing up from my empty plate.

"Everything's set. Noah's parents have offered to get you to the games again this year. That's if you make the team," says Mom, smiling. We both know she's joking. Why wouldn't I make the team?

"That's the thing." I pause. This is going to be even tougher than I thought.

Back when Dad was first diagnosed, my whole world revolved around skates, sticks, helmets, and sweaty locker rooms. Hockey was my life. I didn't care about anything else. I was going to be the next Sidney Crosby. Coach as much as said so. Dad agreed. That was back when Dad was having trouble opening bottles and turning the house key, little things like that. Between all the tests and appointments, we were left scrambling.

"It's important for Sam to keep up with his hockey," Dad said right after the diagnosis came. "This can't come at Sam's expense." Mom got busy making schedules and setting up car-pools, with plans for both of them to come to the rink.

"No worries. We got this," Dad said, smiling. Next, he laid out the rules for living with ALS, all the other things that wouldn't change for us as a family—pizza and movie nights, the Wednesday night Monopoly game.

"What is it, Sam?" Mom asks now, concerned.

Deep breath in. I try again. "I've decided to skip tryouts this year." I look over at Dad. Impossible to tell what he's thinking about the bombshell I just dropped.

"What do you mean, skip tryouts?" Mom glances at Dad. "What's this all about? You love hockey. It's always been hockey. What about your friends?"

Mom's right. Not playing is going to be rough. I don't have many friends outside of hockey. It's been my life for the past nine years. But if I give up hockey it'll be a weight lifted off everyone's shoulders. Dad wasn't able to make it to the ice at all last spring, and what few times Mom was there, it felt like she was losing time with Dad. If it hadn't been for Noah's parents, I wouldn't have even made the games. Every time I came home from a weekend away, the guilt settled in. There's no other way to look at it. Juggling ALS and hockey is wearing our family down. Above all that, there's the financial end of things. Not a problem before Dad got sick, but now it's a totally different story, not that they've said anything to me. But I know. His custom van alone must have cost a ton.

"Maybe I've got some other things going on," I say. Mom raises an eyebrow. I clear my throat. "I could actually use the break," I say, downplaying my decision. I don't want them blaming Dad's illness for this. "And..." I pause, wondering what they'll think. "Right now, I want to concentrate on writing."

"Writing?" Mom looks surprised. I nod, suddenly feeling embarrassed.

Everyone seemed so sure, *I* was so sure, that hockey was it for me. Besides, I've got no time for sports. All the hours I've spent researching ALS, writing my articles, helping out with Dad. Hockey isn't the priority it once was.

"I've been writing some articles for the school blog. Peer pressure, online bullying—stuff like that. Mostly just my opinion about things." Telling them that I'm switching hockey for writing feels weird.

Funny thing is, I didn't even know I could write until I got pissed off by the way some of the girls were treating Jessica Pearce last spring, posting crap about her on Instagram. Not that I knew Jessica personally, but that kind of stuff is just wrong. I decided to do something about it because if you stay quiet then you're no better than the bullies. I wrote a piece about online bullying and it got posted to the blog. People were shocked—they thought that stuff wasn't going on at Forest Glenn. Uh...wrong. Teens are clever. There are plenty of ways for a bully to bully. I kept the article general, didn't use any names, but it hit home. Jim Stakes, the editor-in-chief, said no way was he letting this article be a one-time thing.

"You've got a following," he said. "People are actually reading the blog. We've had tons of hits since we posted that piece you wrote." The day after the article went live, Jessica passed me in the hallway. She didn't smile, but there was this look, you know? Some things don't need to be spoken. They're just understood. I see that all the time with Mom and Dad.

Eyes have a language of their own. Unlike the mouth, which can get you into trouble, the eyes never lie. Dad always said, "Do some good, Sam," and writing that article, seeing the look Jessica gave me, felt good.

"I didn't know we had a writer in the family. Oh Sam, that's wonderful," says Mom, smiling. "And these articles you're writing, it sounds like they'd be relevant for kids your age."

"It keeps me busy," I say. Mom has a habit of overreacting. I see the look on her face and I suddenly wish I hadn't mentioned my writing. What if they want to read my articles? No way am I ready for them to see that part of my life; I'm just figuring it out myself.

"I'm proud of you, Sam," says Dad. "We all have something to offer. We just have to look around and find out what that is. We can all do good."

Well, Dad kind of says it. It's his voice, but he's not speaking. Last month, after that reporter was here, he decided it was time to upload the files he'd recorded while his voice was still strong and start using a speech-generating device, an SGD. With the software on his tablet, he can type out what he wants to say. And there are whole messages that he can access immediately, some of them the corny sayings he was famous for. The other day, I heard him tell Marcie to "Take a chill pill." I used to cringe whenever he said that in front of my friends, but that day, I laughed. I've missed his corniness.

It's nice hearing Dad's real voice, but it's not like having a regular conversation. His pre-recorded messages sound like him, but when he types out a sentence the banked voice is a bit robotic. But, like Mom says, it's been a game changer. It's just taking some getting used to. She teared up when Dad used his banked voice for the first time. She said she missed hearing the sound of his voice.

"The last thing we want is for you to get burned out, Sam." Mom looks over at Dad. "Isn't that right, Gregory?"

"For sure," says Dad. "Do whatever feels right for you."

"I can see you've given this careful consideration," says Mom. I nod. She doesn't say anything for a bit, but then asks again if I'm absolutely sure this is the right move. Maybe she's hoping I won't change my mind.

"I'm positive," I tell her.

She looks at Dad. "Then we'll respect your decision. Won't we, Gregory?"

Dad says, "Absolutely. All we want is for you to be happy. That is the important part."

"But," Mom adds, "you can change your mind when tryouts come around next spring. Decisions can always be reversed. Who knows, maybe by then you'll be anxious to get back on the ice." She smiles and scoops a spoonful of pureed food for Dad.

If things were different, they'd both be fighting me on this. But things aren't different. We're living with ALS—all of us. Only in the end, Dad's the one who'll die from it.

When Dad was first diagnosed, we made a deal that I'd get to all the games and practices, no exceptions. Now, we're pretending that this pause from hockey is legit. Everyone needs a break from time to time. It might even be good for me. Keep me from getting burned out.

We know better, but we're still pretending that my stepping back from this is normal. The thing is, nothing is normal when your life isn't normal.

Gathering my dirty dishes, I put them in the dishwasher. Breaking the news was easier than I thought. Two down, two to go. I'll tell Noah tomorrow. He won't like it, but there'll be lots of hopefuls at tryouts who'll be more than glad to hear I dropped out. I'm not looking forward to telling him, but I owe him that. He should know before I break it to Coach. It won't take long for word to spread.

—

"We're talking Bantam AAA here. You can't just walk away, Sam. We've been dreaming about this a long time. The team needs you." Noah sounds desperate. I feel kind of sorry for him.

"Look, I gave this a lot of thought." Does he think this was easy for me?

"But Sam...you had the most goals *and* assists last season. You're going places. You'd be crazy to quit."

"Mind's made up, man. Accept it and move on." I've got nothing else to say.

"Move on? You can't wake up and decide to quit one day, not after all the hard work we've done. Give me a break."

"Give *you* a break? How about you give *me* a break? Dad's not doing great these days, in case you didn't notice. Mom needs more help—my help. I've got to do my part." Not that I ever thought I'd play the my-dad-has-ALS card, but this whole thing hasn't been easy.

"Look, Sam, you're the best forward we've got. No way we'll make it to the playoffs without you. You drop out and we can kiss the championship goodbye. You'll be letting the whole team down."

Noah's right, spring season *was* good for me, for both of us. Hard to explain. Being out on the ice feels natural, knowing where to position myself for the best play. Noah's always where I need him. No special signals. It happens on its own. We're good together. Still, as good as spring season was, there were times when things felt off. Not that any of the guys noticed—not even Noah. But I missed a few easy plays and that wasn't me. Coach saw and he took me aside.

"What's the problem, Sam? You seem distracted," he said. Dad had just gotten out of the hospital and there were all these new instructions for his care. I was worried how Mom was making out with me being gone. So, when Coach asked what was going on, I spilled my guts. He shook his head and said, "Tough break, kid," and I wished I hadn't told him. Not sure what I was expecting. I said I'd pull it together, and I did, but it wasn't easy.

"Come on—what do you say? Just another season. Just one more. You'll get through it. Maybe things will get better after that. We'll get to check this year—it's what we've been waiting for." I shake my head. Nothing he says will change my mind. As for things getting better, Noah's dreaming. There is no *better* with ALS.

"Back off, Noah. I've gotta do this. Respect my decision. Mom and Dad are."

He swats my arm. "Smarten up, Sam. I know your dad's sick, but no way are you quitting hockey."

He thinks I'm putting him on. I look him square in the eye. For a few moments we stare at each other, the way we do when we're out on the ice, anticipating the next move. It hits me in the gut. If *he's* disappointed, how does he think *I* feel? I'm the one giving it all up, not him.

Noah starts to say something but then stops. The look in his eye. He finally gets it. I'm dead serious. I've never seen him look so bummed out before. Except maybe that first year we went for tryouts and he didn't make the team. When he found out he wasn't on the roster, I didn't think he'd be able to hold it together. It seemed like the end of the world for both of us.

But staying down never changes a thing. We worked on his game till he got better and the next time he made the team. One thing he's right about. We've been waiting to get to this level for more competitive play, to see how we make out with the bigger guys. It's all we've talked about for years. So, yeah, it sucks, and I get that, but making tough decisions always does.

CHAPTER 3

A FEW DAYS BEFORE TRYOUTS START, I GET HAULED into Sandford's office. I was just in to see her a few days back, so I'm pretty sure Coach put her up to it when he didn't make any headway with Mom and Dad on the phone the other night. I overheard Mom say she was respecting my decision and that he should too.

Coach probably thinks I'm at the breaking point and that Mom and Dad are out to lunch for letting me quit. No one in their right mind would drop out of the game, especially someone with my potential—at least, that's probably how he sees it. Wish he'd get that walking away from hockey is tough enough without everyone trying to talk me out of it. It's been my life since I was five. Not just the fact that I'm not playing, but the guys seem different these days. Even Noah. I'm an outsider now. It's not like I'll even be going to the games and cheering them on.

Ms. Sandford's office is inside the Rainbow Room. It's the safest place in the school for kids to hang out. I started coming here a few weeks before the spring hockey session, but only because Mom insisted.

"I can see that things are hard for you, Sam. You need someone to talk to. A professional," Mom said. "Not just your dad and me." She was right, things were tough. Dad was in the hospital and Mom was spending a lot of her time there.

"I'm okay. Really. Exercise releases endorphins, the feel-good hormone," I said, repeating something I'd heard in school. "Once hockey's over, I can stay active. I'll take up jogging." I wanted her to know that she could depend on me—they both could. But Mom put her hand up. She didn't want to hear what I was saying.

"I've spoken to Ms. Sandford and she agrees. You have an appointment with her tomorrow morning at ten thirty. It's non-negotiable." And just like that I got roped into these meetings. Twice-a-month check-in, Sandford calls them.

"What's up?" Noah asked when he saw me coming out of the Rainbow Room after that first meeting. Figures I'd run into Noah of all people. What were the chances of him being in that end of the school? It's not like he has any classes there.

"Mom's idea," I said, making it sound like it was nothing.

After that, the guys on the team started asking what the deal was. Athletes aren't supposed to have any worries or anxiety.

"Does your Mom know she's making you look like a wee-nie?" Chuck laughed.

"Lay off," I told him. Noah and his big mouth. If I could have gotten out of coming to Sandford's office, don't they think I would have? I knew the guys on the team would give me a hard time when they found out. Exactly the reason I didn't want to go.

But then, I saw it wasn't all bad. I even got the idea to write a blog post about the Rainbow Room. Like me, I figured most of the kids didn't really understand what it was all about. No one I knew hung out here. Turns out all those colours and rainbows aren't so weird after all. It's just a safe place for kids to go and be themselves. No matter what that is. In the Rainbow Room, acceptance is the number one rule, which I put in the blog post. I even got permission to upload some photos so readers could see what a cool place it is. All sorts of kids come here, not just the artsy types. There's this one guy, Henry, who's really into science. The things he knows are mind-blowing. Two girls from the student council decided to check it out because of the article I wrote. I see them here all the time now. And athletes come too. There's Adan and Will, players from the basketball team. It's not just a place for ex-hockey players.

I settle into one of the chairs while waiting for Ms. Sandford and check out the framed photos on the walls for the hundredth time, colourful art made by some of the kids—past and present. There's a mural on one wall with a yellow-brick road. A large rainbow sweeps overhead. The trees look like lollipops and the flowers are every colour imaginable. A collage of framed pictures is on the wall opposite the mural. Pretty cool. I recognized one of the paintings the first day I came here. The artist went to Forest Glenn and now shows their work in some pretty famous galleries. There was an article about them in one of Mom's magazines. There's an Inclusion Board at the front of the room that kids can add to—art, quotes, a sentence saying what they want others to know about them. It gets changed up every few months.

The sign behind Ms. Sandford's desk has a Ralph Waldo Emerson quote that reads *Be silly, be honest, be kind.* Sandford's cool. She's got a good rep with the kids. She's fair and she listens, but she's tough when she needs to be.

A few moments later, she breezes into the room. Her purple hair looks a bit messy. She lowers herself in her chair and pulls herself up to her desk. Her hands are clasped in front of her. She starts out by asking how things are at home. I tell her okay, but she keeps at it.

"It can't be easy, your dad having ALS. You helping out with his care. Is there anything new going on?" she says. I shake my head. The voice bank Dad's using is still pretty new, but I haven't mentioned it yet. What's the point?

"Maybe you'd like to talk about the challenges in being a caregiver—all the responsibilities that come with it," says Ms. Sandford.

She never tiptoes around ALS. I like that. I'm tired of people acting as if I'll come unhinged at the mention of Dad's illness. I shrug. I've got to say something.

"I don't really do much. I just hang out at the house so Mom can get a break. We talk about things and sometimes he needs me to get stuff for him. Mom's the real caregiver. Dad pretty much can't be left alone these days."

Three years ago, Dad and I made a list of the things I wouldn't have to do when times got tough. Diapers, catheters, and sponge baths were all tied for number one. Followed by drool.

"We'll leave all diapers unchanged," he said while making the list. It sounded funny at the time; now, not so much.

"All that takes away time you could be spending with your friends or just doing other things." Ms. Sandford keeps pressing. "How do you feel about that?"

I shift in my seat. Didn't we go through all this a few months back? "He's my dad. I do what I have to." Some of the guys wanted me to hang out at the mall with them last Saturday. I wish they'd stop asking. Saying no is brutal. I've told them before, Mom has coffee with her friends on Saturdays—the faithful three, she calls them. Like Mom, they're all caregivers. It's why they formed their group. Only my friends keep forgetting.

Sandford nods. "Love. Loyalty. Responsibility. Guilt. They go hand in hand. I get that. A lot of feelings going on all at once."

She's got that right. Just wish she'd get off of this and talk about something else. I'm not in the mood.

"I've heard you're giving up hockey," she says finally. I was wondering when *that* was going to come up. Confirms what I thought about Coach putting her up to this.

"Why does everyone think I can't make my own decisions?" I didn't mean to raise my voice. I'm quick to apologize.

"All of us, we just want to make sure this is what you really want, that you've thought it through. No regrets later." She smiles.

"Well, everyone can stop being concerned. I'm fine."

We make eye contact. She's deciding if I'm telling the truth.

"You *do* know where I am. Anytime you need to talk. And I mean that," she says. "You don't have to go through this alone."

We chat a bit more about unimportant things. She brings up that stupid hat Pharrell Williams is wearing everywhere and the mood quickly changes.

"When you've got the number one hit, you can probably wear whatever you want." That hat is ridiculous, but it's getting him loads of publicity.

"'Happy'—now how can you go wrong with a title like that?" says Sandford.

"Probably can't."

"I don't have a number one song, but I wouldn't mind having a hat like his," says Ms. Sandford. I laugh. I can totally see that.

"Just a thought," says Ms. Sandford before I head off to class. "Have you considered keeping a record of your journey with your dad's Lou Gehrig's? You might want to look back on it all one day."

Keep a record? She's got to be kidding. I won't want to remember any of this later. I shake my head. The bell rings and I take off.

ALS, a.k.a. Lou Gehrig's disease. Three years ago, I didn't know who Lou Gehrig was, let alone the disease named after him. But I've been digging around online. Lou Gehrig played for the New York Yankees. He was one of the greatest base-ball players of all time. Triple Crown winner, All-Star seven times in a row, American League MVP a couple of times, plus a member of six World Series champion teams. Inducted into the Baseball Hall of Fame in 1939. He had everything going for him. But just like that, his career got cut short because of amyotrophic lateral sclerosis. He had to retire at thirty-six. That's just nuts. No one has to retire at thirty-six. To top it all off, he died two years later. What a freaking waste.

I head down the hallway thinking about Dad and the thousand Canadians diagnosed every year with ALS, and everyone who's going to die from it this year. All of it, a waste.

CHAPTER 4

IT'S THE FIRST DAY OF TRYOUTS. CLOSED TO THE PUB-
lic, but I'm not really the public. I stride through the parking lot, pull open the back door, and slip inside the arena,
unnoticed. The smells hit me first—chemicals, rubber floor-
ing. And that chill in the air. There's a feeling you get at ice
level. The anticipation. The energy. It's hard to describe.

The cutting in of skates, the slap of the sticks, the puck off
the boards, hitting the goal posts—warm-up sounds. I move
closer. The ice is full of hopefuls showing off their moves.
Not so long ago that was me. I glance around quickly, see
five evaluators sitting in random seats throughout the arena.
They're holding clipboards, taking notes. Watching. Judging.
Deciding which players to cut. It's brutal, and the pressure
is intense. Everyone wanting to do their best—better than
best—knowing they're being watched. Noah and me always
showed up super early just to impress them. That's the key.
Getting noticed by the right people—standing out from the
pack. Now, I'm just an observer. I step up closer to the glass.
Why am I even here? I should go home. I kick at the boards,
reminded again that life sucks big time. And for the millionth
time, I wonder: Why ALS? Why us?

A group of guys speed past; Noah's one of them. I know
Noah. He's a bundle of nerves. There's a number 5 on his
pinny. That's my number—the one I always hope for. What
are the chances? When he sees me standing behind the glass,

he slows. Our eyes lock. He wants to come over. He thinks I've changed my mind. But he realizes pretty quickly I'm just watching. Chuck skates by and taps Noah's shin pad with his stick. One last look and Noah speeds across the ice. He turns and starts skating backwards. He's fast. Skating backwards is his speciality skill. He's solid and strong and faster than the guys skating forward. It's what makes him an outstanding D-man. The evaluators will be impressed. They look for speed—backwards and forwards. But more than that, they want to see focus and attitude, leadership; all things Coach told me I had. It was how I made captain.

I check the time. I'd best get going. But then I get this weird feeling; there's someone standing beside me. I glance across. It's Coach. He nods. I want to say something but don't. We look away and watch the ice for a while, saying nothing, thinking everything. The space around us is super awkward. I know he's got something on his mind and it's got to do with my decision. He's not happy I quit. He called the house again last night and Mom had him on speakerphone so Dad could hear.

Coach needs to understand. I didn't make this decision overnight. As great as the spring hockey session was, it was equally brutal—two practices a week and full games every weekend all over the Atlantic region. With everything going on at home, I could barely keep up with it all. I was stupid to think I could pull it off.

If Coach thought I was having problems keeping my head in the game last spring, the fall session wouldn't be any better. Spring session was eight weeks long and I struggled to stay on top. But this? September through March? There are too many things to think about. Too much time away from home, not to mention the cost. Two and a half years into the disease, Mom quit her job to look after Dad. I don't want to add to the burden for her. Besides, Mom needs me. Marcie can't be there all the time, and Dad's only getting sicker. He's going to need more and more care. ALS is a progressive disease.

Before he lost his voice, I heard him tell Marcie that he doesn't want a ventilator. I know what that means and it scares the crap out of me.

Coach clears his throat. I wait for the lecture that's coming. "Things still rough at home, Sam?"

"Could be better," I say—a complete understatement. I scuff my sneaker against the floor. Things won't get any better, but no one seems to get that.

"Look, kid, I've told you this in the past, you're an up-and-comer. You could go places. You know that, don't you?" I look at the floor. Some of the players find Coach intimidating, all of them respect him. He's a good guy. He doesn't just care about winning.

"I've talked with your parents a few times. They say it's your decision. I know things are rough, but do you realize what you're giving up here?" I nod. "Are your folks okay with it? I mean *really* okay?" I nod again. I actually think they were relieved. One less thing to juggle. It was different when Dad could come to the rink. The last time was a year ago. Now it's out of the question.

"I hate to see you fire it all away."

I continue to casually kick at the floor, shaking my head. He's not going to talk me out of it. "Who knows? It might just be for a season or two." Juggling hockey with my dad's life expectancy feels messed up on every level imaginable.

"There's still time for you to change your mind. You know that, kid?" I nod. He places a firm hand on my shoulder and leaves me standing there behind the glass, looking out at the ice. I want to smash something right now. Should have known better than to show up today.

I turn to leave. The sounds of skates digging into the ice, the pucks off the boards and posts, follow me. As I push my way out the back door, the coaching staff is calling the players together. They're getting started. It would be easy to get my gear and join them. So frigging easy.

I hesitate, then keep on going.

CHAPTER 5

A FEW DAYS LATER, I SPOT JON AND A BUNCH OF THE guys in the cafeteria.

"Sam! Noah!" Jon raises his arm. "Over here." I let Jon know we'll be there in a sec and grab a tray.

"Are they talking?" I ask Noah.

"Last year's star player doesn't show up for the first round of tryouts—are you kidding me?"

Noah's right. What was I thinking? I grab some food and wait for the lunch lady to ring it in. The guys are laughing about something. They're always goofing around.

As we close in on them, I hear Chuck replaying something that happened out on the ice, maybe during tryouts. I set my tray down and slide into a seat. Noah sits across from me. Suddenly, Chuck stops speaking and looks at me, like maybe I won't want to hear.

I take my sandwich out of the wrapper. "Keep going," I tell him. I'm genuinely interested. He's funny. Chuck blows off the rest of his story, barely making it to the punchline, which doesn't get a single laugh; nearly unheard of for Chuck. There's a moment of awkward silence. I ask how try-outs went. It'll be a while before they announce the roster. They look at me like I shouldn't be asking.

"What's up? Do I have cooties or something?" I say, hoping to lighten things up. No one even cracks a smile. The guys look over at Jon, as if he's the official spokesperson.

"We thought you might not want to talk about hockey," he says.

"What do you mean? Why wouldn't I?"

"Because…" He shrugs. "You know." He looks over at Noah, but Noah stays quiet. I'm glad. This isn't something he can help with. Jon mumbles something about Dad being sick. I wish everyone would stop saying that. Things are rough, but they can still joke around with me.

"It's just hockey," I tell Jon—all of them. "It's not like someone died." I give a weird laugh and reach for my milk.

Silence. They're all looking at me like I'm nuts. Saying it's "just hockey" to these guys is an insult. It's never been "just hockey" for any of us. I know better.

"Sorry, man. I didn't mean anything." I take another bite of my sandwich.

I stop paying attention to what the guys are talking about after that and concentrate on eating. I didn't mean to tick them off. But them feeling sorry for me, that's not cool either.

I zone out and start thinking about an idea I had the other night for a blog post. Is Forest Glenn even ready for it? Am *I* ready for it? I emailed my idea to Jim the other night but he hasn't gotten back to me. Jim has an open mind. Important for an editor. The blog is student run. Anyone in the school can submit articles and story ideas, though it doesn't all get posted. Sometimes ideas have to be run past Ms. Sandford, to make sure the content is appropriate. I get that. Until recently, most of those ideas were about athletics, music, and fashion. Not things like personal freedom or bullying. And for sure, not the idea I fired off in my email.

When Noah and I leave the cafeteria, the guys are still at the table. They're joking around again, back to sounding like themselves.

"That went well," I say to Noah as we head to our lockers.

"What did you expect?" He looks at me as if to say I know better, and I do.

I grab my backpack. Feels weird, what just happened. The guys think I let them down. I'm pretty sure Noah does too, but he'll get over it in time. At least, I hope he will. As for the rest of them, I can't be sure—Jon, maybe. I look down the hallway, people getting ready for class. I wonder how many of them have heard I dropped out of hockey. Is it even a talked-about thing or something just the guys know? I close my locker. I've got to stay focused. As Dad used to say, "What you think of me isn't my business"—a blog post for another day? Maybe.

I punch Noah in the arm. "Catch up with you later," I say before heading off to find Jim.

There's a utility closet next to Mr. Rushton's room. *Home of Forest Glenn Blog* is on the door. It's open, so I know Jim's still there. He's slipping his backpack on when I arrive.

"I know why you're here," he says, "and I like it. I sent it off to Sandford. She just got back to me. She says she'll need to see the article before it's posted."

"So, it's a go?"

Jim nods. "For now, at least. Sandford gets final approval, so watch yourself. It could get tricky if it's not handled the right way. You'll do rewrites if she asks?"

"Censorship?"

"Get real, man. It's a school blog." He closes the door, then turns toward me. "Write about what's going on with your dad. Use Stephen Hawking as an example, just like you said in your email. Everyone's heard of him. Maybe explain how ALS isn't just about the Ice Bucket Challenge we did last summer. Make it real. It's okay to mention Kevorkian, but don't make him the main focus of the post. Got it?" He closes the door.

The bell rings and I head off to class.

CHAPTER 6

"MAKE ROOM FOR THE BOSS MAN," SAYS MARCIE, barrelling her way out of Dad's room. I hear the motor from Dad's powerchair and then he appears in the doorway. He makes his way into the living room and Marcie closes the door behind him. It's early in the day and already Dad looks tired. I hope today doesn't end up being too much for him. But he is determined to go.

Long before ALS came to our family, Dad was into the idea of "dying with dignity." Not for *him*, but in general. It started after Grandpa Gillis got sick. We'd go to the hospital to visit. The last time we went, Grandpa's eyes were sunken, his mouth a round wrinkled O. He was lying so still. Snow white sheets made his skin look dark.

"Won't make it this time," he whispered. I'm not even sure who he was talking to. They had taken his teeth out and he looked ancient. Dad reached out and held his hand. His fingernails looked like they'd been dipped in bleach, so white and shrivelled. I stood by the bed, frozen, watching Grandpa's mouth sucking air in and out. His eyes moved back and forth beneath the thin skin of his eyelids. When he finally stopped sucking in air, a strange look came over Dad's face.

"Where's the dignity?" he said to Mom later.

After Grandpa died, I had nightmares about that wrinkled round O. I was maybe seven at the time. I haven't really thought of him since all of this stuff started with Dad.

There's a Dying with Dignity demonstration planned in front of the Nova Scotia Legislature today at noon. Dad asked Marcie to take him down. Truthfully, it didn't take much convincing. Marcie agrees that people should have the right to choose the way their life ends when they're terminally ill. I wanted to go to the rally too. It's important, and Dad agreed. "A good experience," he said.

Mom's out running errands; if she were home she'd put a stop to this. Never mind the fact that I ditched school to take part in today's rally. She'd say I'm too young. She'd never approve. Dad, Marcie, and I all know it. Dad has never been one to sit on the sidelines and let things happen, and part of me is kind of glad that hasn't changed. When he heard about today's rally, he was determined to go. Nothing new for him. Only today's rally is personal. You could even say it's a matter of life and death.

When Dying with Dignity Canada opened a chapter in Nova Scotia last year, Dad became involved. Just one more thing on his list of volunteer work.

Not long after the diagnosis, I overheard him on the phone. I thought he'd let all that volunteer stuff go, concentrate on himself for once.

"'The city needs affordable housing," he was saying to someone. "Well, maybe we all need to step up. There are people living in tents. Did you hear me? Tents...Because I saw it...The other day...There are always going to be flaws in the system, but we keep working to make things better, not give up because of it." He was raising his voice, something he didn't often do. His lawyer buddies thought he shouldn't work for free, which made him more determined. That's my dad, always fighting for justice. Not even ALS can take that from him.

"All set?" says Marcie, looking at Dad. I like the bright red and blue headband she's wearing, her dark brown hair sticking up straight. She wears it super short, but lately she's been letting it grow, which adds about three inches to her height. She's wearing red lipstick. I guess maybe she's trying to stand out in the crowd. Marcie doesn't hold anything back. Olivia says she's a what-you-see-is-what-you-get kind of gal.

"It's what attracted me to her," Olivia said when she introduced Marcie to us the first time. That was last winter when Mom finally admitted she needed help with Dad's care. Olivia said her partner would be perfect for the job. "Just don't ask for her opinion if you don't want to know the truth," she added. Olivia was right about that.

I hurry to the garage to get the signs I made. I hold them up to show Marcie and Dad.

"I'll take that one," Marcie says, pointing to the sign that reads, *Freedom of Choice.*

"Great job," says Dad. He wanted his sign to say, *The Choice Should Be Mine.*

The last one, the one I'll be carrying, is short and to the point: *Right to Die.*

I gather up the bag with the snacks and bottled water, and grab the signs. But before we can make it out the door, the phone rings. I toss the signs onto the couch and hurry to see who's calling in case it's Mom. *UNKNOWN CALLER.* I let it ring. Shoot. It's probably the school checking to see where I am. That's how Noah and I got caught skipping once before, that and Noah's big mouth. They'll leave a message, but I can delete it after I get home.

"No one important," I say, grabbing up the signs again.

"All set?" says Marcie, looking first at Dad and then me. I nod. Determination settles in as we head for the front door. At least it feels like we're doing something, not just sitting back and letting ALS take control.

I lower the ramp for the van and Dad drives on in. While I put the signs in the back, Marcie locks the powerchair in place.

"Ready for takeoff," says Dad as she turns the ignition.

Marcie manoeuvres the van through traffic like a pro. She doesn't mind driving Dad around, not even at rush hour. She stays as cool as a cucumber. I sometimes wonder if anything ever fazes this woman. Give her any disaster—earthquake, alien invasion, zombie apocalypse—and she'd likely come out the other side smiling. When she first came to help out, she refused to drive the van, said it was too big and awkward. It wasn't long before she was sitting behind the wheel, honking at pedestrians, and whispering curse words at the other drivers, occasionally flipping them the bird. A madwoman behind the wheel, I call her, which I think she likes.

"It's nice weather. The sun feels good," says Dad, and Marcie agrees.

Marcie backs the van out of the driveway and puts it in gear.

I can see Dad's face in the side-view mirror. Wish I knew what was really going through his mind, not just his thoughts on the weather. On second thought, scratch that. I can do without knowing.

"Let's take the scenic route," says Marcie, putting the blinker on. "The rally starts at twelve, so we've got plenty of time. Your father needs some legal papers picked up anyway."

Dad used to go down to the Legal Aid building all the time. Now, he works from home. As long as he can move his right hand to use the keyboard, he'll keep on working. After that, I don't know.

"Hard to believe this street turned two hundred and fifty last month," she says, turning down Gottingen. "They had a big to-do a while ago. Interviewed people to get their stories about growing up here." Marcie's up on pretty much everything that's happening in the city. She glances in the rear-view mirror at Dad.

I look out the window and absently ask if she had a story to tell. Seriously, I could see her giving an interview, babbling away to someone she doesn't know.

"Not likely."

We turn off Gottingen and down Russell Street.

I stay in the van with Dad while Marcie goes into the Legal Aid building. He doesn't say anything and neither do I. Again, I wonder what's going through his mind. Is he thinking about his hope of making a difference in the world and what will happen when he's unable to volunteer? Or is he thinking about the rally today and what this legislation could mean for him?

"Find a cause, Sam, and do some good in the world," he used to tell me. I never thought the decriminalization of medically assisted death was something I'd get behind. It's a heavy load. Dad wants changes made. He wants to know that it will be legal, if the time ever comes and he's just too tired to keep up the fight. But there's more to his thoughts on this whole issue. People don't always wait for something to become legal before doing it.

I think about the articles I've been writing for the school blog. I'm not sure they're making a difference in the world or if it's just that writing them makes me feel better. Dad has supported a lot of causes over the years. What I don't get is why life decided it didn't need his help anymore.

But today at the rally things are different; every voice counts, including Dad's.

Marcie turns down Hollis Street. The legislature is just up ahead. She slows to a snail's pace. I scan the area for wheelchair-accessible parking. No luck. All the spots are taken. A crowd has already gathered in front of Province House. Maybe this will be bigger than I thought.

"Keep driving," I tell Marcie. "Did you really think finding a place to park down here would be easy?"

"Miracles happen," she says sarcastically and continues on to the parkade.

She finally gets the van parked. We'll have to walk back, but that's no biggie.

"Come on, sunshine." Marcie opens the door to the van.

I release the locks on Dad's chair and lower the ramp.

"All set?" she asks once he's outside.

"I'm ready to roll," says Dad.

"Then let's get to it," says Marcie.

CHAPTER 7

I STUFF THE SNACKS AND WATER BOTTLES IN THE basket on Dad's wheelchair. Not that Dad eats snacks these days, since his food is pureed, but Marcie insisted, saying that food and water were essential for any rally.

"Since you're a seasoned activist, I'll take your word for it," I tell her. She doesn't say anything, just gives me this knowing smile. I bet she's got a lot of protest stories to tell. She's been a volunteer for the Rainbow Action Project since before I was born. She's used to rallies. I wonder what it would be like to have to fight just to be who you are.

"The snacks might be an added bonus. You know—in case we get thrown in jail," she says, grinning.

"Jail? You're kidding me, right?"

"Maybe we need a cake with a nail file, in case we have to break out. What do think, boss man?" She nudges Dad.

"Highly unlikely," he says.

"More like you not passing up snacks," I say. Dad laughs.

Marcie shoots me a look. But I know it's put on. I get the signs out of the van and fasten Dad's to the back of his power-chair where it can be seen. I fold the ramp back in place, give him a thumbs up, and shut the door.

Dad takes off in the direction of the legislature building with what I like to think is a look of determination. Truthfully, he doesn't have much facial expression; just another symptom of the disease.

We follow as Dad leads the way. He got the chair two years ago when his then wobbly legs started to let him down more and more. A black eye and dislocated shoulder later, he gave in and agreed to the chair. He's doing okay with it for now, but I think about what will happen when he can't work the joystick on his own. The way things are going, that could be anytime. Dad hates depending upon others. He does what he's capable of. Some days that's more than others. I used to think that if I were him, I'd let people wait on me hand and foot. But not Dad. The day his chair arrived, he said it was perfect because it had a five-year warranty.

"I'll be long gone before the warranty gives out."

I could see in Mom's eyes she didn't think that was funny; it was something she didn't want to think about. Neither of us did. I'm not sure how Dad could joke about it, but sometimes a sense of humour gets you through the day.

There are a lot of people on the sidewalk. I've got to give Dad credit, he's super good at manoeuvring his wheelchair. People look at him, and then at the sign he's toting. *Way to go, Dad*. It's cool seeing him move through the crowd like that. People step aside for him as he motors down the sidewalk, some nod. I look around. "There must be at least a hundred people," I say.

"And more coming," says Marcie. Before we left today, she said we'd be lucky if a few dozen show up. She looks at me and smiles. I know what she's thinking. Seeing the number of people here feels like a small win.

Many of the people are holding signs supporting the Dying with Dignity cause; older or middle-aged, people with greying hair. Some have caregivers with them, like Dad.

There are a few police officers milling around—a precaution and something to be expected during a rally, even a peaceful one. The Charter of Rights and Freedoms gives us the right to assembly so that rallies like this are even possible. Dad made me read up on it before I came. Mostly because he's a lawyer and everything with him is about the law. Not that today's rally is illegal. It's all legit. The Dying with Dignity group is about legalizing doctor-assisted death. People have been fighting for it for a long time—well, fighting for *and* fighting against.

"It's not about dying," Dad said one day before he lost his voice. "It's about choice. When you know you're going to die, you should have the choice to do it peacefully and without pain. Why should anyone tell me what to do with my own body? It's ludicrous." By the looks of the crowd today, a lot of other people feel the same way.

Someone is setting up a camera, getting ready to record— the evening news, from what I can tell. I'm impressed that the media is here.

"Maybe the right people will start getting the message," says Marcie as we walk past a woman holding a microphone. I know by *the right people* she means government. We've had these discussions before. Having the media here is a good first step. I walk through the crowd, looking at the people, wondering what each one's story is.

Suddenly, there's a microphone in front of me. It takes a few seconds for it to register that the woman is speaking to me.

"What brings you out today? You seem young to have taken up the Dying with Dignity cause." I look up at her, stunned. What am I supposed to say?

I start out with "I...er...um..." and sound less than intelligent, but then I quickly get a grip. I've spent plenty of time doing research. I'm better than this.

I take a deep breath and begin. "My dad was diagnosed with ALS three years ago." Oh wow, did that just sound weird. I'm not used to talking to strangers about all this, especially not with a microphone stuck in my face. I take another breath and keep going. It's important. "We've talked about this—as a family. We put our pets out of their misery when they're suffering, but governments won't allow us to choose that same option for ourselves." The reporter is nodding. She gets what I'm saying. I can tell she's impressed that I'm not just a brainless teen looking to get an afternoon off school.

School—it hits me then. My stomach drops. No way am I not getting busted for this. Maybe I can tell the reporter not to air the interview, to skip over what I just said. I spin around to stop her, but it's too late.

"What brings *you* down to the legislature today?" she says to someone behind me. And just like that, she's moved on. I can't just butt in while they're recording.

I look at Marcie in desperation. What was I thinking? This will make the evening news for sure. She shrugs. "Next time, kid, try saying, 'no comment.' Works for me every time." No sympathy.

"If this makes the six o'clock news, I'm dead. Mom will have a conniption." A conniption? Am I seventy-five? Clearly I've been hanging out with Marcie too long.

Some people have walked up the steps of the legislature where a microphone has been set up. Marcie and Dad are glued to what's going on, waiting for someone to speak. They couldn't care less about me. I tug on Marcie's arm to get her attention.

"You know, she'll blast Dad for bringing me here," I say. Still nothing. "And you—she'll blame you too, Marcie," I put in for good measure. Marcie raises an eyebrow.

"I just work for your parents," she says. "I do what I'm told."

Police officers are mingling through the protesters; some stop to talk. All in all, everything is pretty low-key. A woman walks over to the microphone and starts speaking. She says how important it is for terminally ill people to have a say in what their end of life will be like.

"Needless suffering for someone who will eventually die from their disease is cruel," she says and the people clap. She says 84 percent of Canadians agree that a doctor should be able to help someone end their life if they are competent and terminally ill and suffering unbearably.

"So why, in 2014, is it not law?" Again, everyone claps, and what she is saying makes sense—all things I've heard Mom and Dad talk about.

"Now, if the government would get the lead out," says Marcie, looking first at Dad and then me while she claps. "Bills take forever to get passed in parliament."

The woman on the steps waits for the clapping to die down before speaking again. Just as she begins, someone in the crowd starts shouting. Voices behind me join together. It takes a while for what's going on to sink in. I look around to see who's doing the shouting. The woman pauses, but then keeps speaking into the microphone, this time louder, as she tries to make herself heard over the hecklers. A small group of people step forward. I can't quite make out what's being said. Eventually it becomes clear.

"United for Life." "All life is precious." They raise signs, their voices echoing through the pack. More people with signs join the crowd in front of the legislature. The numbers are growing.

A man with a *Support Dying with Dignity* sign starts calling out to the protesters, telling them to go home. He walks toward them, shouting louder. This could get serious. I don't want anyone getting hurt, especially not Dad.

People on both sides are now yelling at one another. The woman at the mic tells everyone to stay calm.

"This is not what this rally is about," she says. No one is listening. Someone with an *All Life is Precious* sign knocks into me—hard. The signboard they're carrying almost clips me in the back of the head and I duck.

"Are you okay?" Marcie looks concerned.

I nod.

"Let's skedaddle," she says in a serious tone. I look at Dad and then at Marcie. I mean—seriously? This was supposed to be a peaceful rally, to raise awareness for a good cause.

We turn toward where the van is parked. There are a lot of people in front of us, blocking our way to the parkade.

Inching our way through the crowd is next to impossible.

"Please step aside." I'm practically begging them to move out of the way. No one is budging. What's wrong with these guys? Can't they hear? A man hurrying past us bumps into Dad's wheelchair. There's a wild look in his eye as he glances at Dad then to the sign fastened to the back of his chair. Scowling, the man turns his sign around so it is facing us. *Assisted Dying is Still Murder,* it says. Things are getting weird. Marcie's right. We've got to get out of here. Someone's got to do something. Quick.

I look around. Where's a police officer when you want one? I glare out at the crowd.

"Let us through," I say. "We want...we *need* to get through." People are shouting. Give me a break. Can't they see someone could get hurt? I don't give in. I keep telling them to make way. I finally yell as loud as I can, "My dad could get hurt. Now move it!"

The crowd slowly steps aside, giving us room. Dad's wheelchair burns rubber—as much as a wheelchair can—as we head back toward the van. He's not wasting any time. Good thing he's strapped in. The sidewalk is bumpy and he could get tossed. Behind us, people are still shouting at one another. We get Dad inside the van and Marcie jumps behind the wheel. More police officers are moving in, seconds before I slide the door shut and climb into the passenger seat.

"What just happened back there? So much for peaceful rallies," says Marcie as she pulls out of the parking space. She sounds upset, and I take back what I said earlier about nothing fazing her. She's clearly fazed.

"People on both sides want to be heard," says Dad.

As we pull out of the parkade, though, I feel a sudden surge of pleasure. Things were pretty tense for a while, but it sure beat the quiet rally outside the legislature that was planned. Those protesters just drew more attention to the cause—dumbasses.

I can't help it. I start laughing.

"What's with you?" says Marcie, looking across at me.

"At least we didn't get arrested. Isn't that right?" I say, looking over my shoulder at Dad.

"Dad with ALS spends night in jail. Caregiver causes a commotion. Snacks confiscated," says Dad. Marcie lets out a grunt. "Listen to the two of you. Someone could have gotten hurt."

"We didn't, and the bonus is we didn't need a file to break out of jail." I can barely hold it in. Dad is laughing too.

"Laugh now—the both of you. Think your mother's not going to hear about this?" says Marcie, looking across at me.

"You weren't worried when the reporter nabbed me." In fact, she blew me off, basically told me I should have kept my mouth shut.

"The minute things get rough, the media jumps all over it. They'll take this and run with it," says Marcie, stepping on the gas.

CHAPTER 8

BY THE TIME WE PULL UP TO THE HOUSE, MARCIE'S mood has lightened. The driveway's empty, meaning Mom's not home.

"I want to rest," says Dad.

This afternoon wiped him out, but I know he's glad he went. I take the signs from the van and put them in the garage, then remove the SGD from the wheelchair and attach it to the floor mount in his room. We barely have him settled in bed when Mom comes through the front door.

She calls out a cheery "I'm home, guys," and heads straight for Dad's room. It's always her first stop when she gets back from doing errands.

"How did the rally go?" she asks Dad.

"It was interesting," I hear him say before Mom closes his bedroom door.

"Interesting? That's one way of putting it," says Marcie as she packs up to leave. She stops before reaching the door. Grinning, she adds, "See you on the six o'clock news."

Nothing like rubbing it in. "Thanks a lot, Marcie."

"Good luck, kid. You're probably going to need it," she says moments before closing the door.

While Mom's talking to Dad, I get rid of the voicemail the school left this morning. I'll remind Dad to email and let them know he's aware of my absence. Now all I have to do is keep Mom from watching the six o'clock news.

Satisfied that I've covered all my bases for now, I head off to my room to play some Xbox. I hate being deceitful, but sometimes it's necessary. Mom's got enough going on without her worrying about me. One missed day of school isn't the end of the world. And like Dad said, it was supposed to be a good experience for me.

"Dinner smells good," says Dad, coming to the table. I wonder how pureed chicken tastes. I like that we always eat dinner together and talk about our day. At least some things haven't changed.

Mom's in a really good mood at the moment. She's telling us how the woman on cash at the grocery store recognized her from the newspaper article back when we did the Ice Bucket Challenge. Watching Mom and Dad together right now, I start wondering what will happen when Dad's not able to swallow. Mom had a dietitian speak to him about getting a feeding tube to help him get his nutrients. He said he'd consider it when the time came. I figured that meant "no way."

The time came six months later when he was having trouble swallowing his medication. Right now, the tube is only for water and meds. Mom expected that he'd get his nutrients that way too. But I'd once heard him say he didn't want to prolong the inevitable. That means no feeding tubes to get his nutrition, and no invasive ventilation.

The no ventilation part is going to be a tough one for all of us. Dad signed an advance directive saying everything he did and didn't want to happen with his healthcare in the future. Being a lawyer, he made sure all the proper paperwork was done.

"It's not right to put you in that position," he told Mom.

I keep the conversation going through dinner by asking lots of questions every time a subject comes up. Mom likes that. She says asking questions is how we learn new things. Dad mentions a movie being filmed in Halifax, something Marcie told him about, and they talk about that for a while. I'm not sure if Dad knows what I'm up to, but if we can drag dinner out a while longer, I should be in the clear—the local news usually airs first. With any luck she won't find out I went to the rally. On the other hand, maybe I'm dreaming.

I bring up an idea I have for a future article for the school blog—what it takes to run for class president with the election coming up soon—and we talk about that for a bit. Eventually she gets around to asking about my day.

"Same old," I say, not looking up from my plate. I stab a piece of broccoli and shove it in my mouth, hoping I don't look like I have something to hide. At least I know Dad's not going to let anything slip. I quickly mention the government's plan I heard about for renewable energy, a subject Mom's really behind. Pretty soon, the conversation moves to greenhouse gas emissions and what will happen in the future if we don't get our heads out of our own butts.

Once dinner's over, I offer to put the dishes in the dish-washer. When I'm finished, I come out of the kitchen and round the corner in time to see my face on the TV screen. I should have kept her talking in the kitchen longer. Only I got so wrapped up in the conversation, I forgot to check the time. I look at Mom. She stares at me, then looks over at Dad.

"Gregory, you were in on this?"

"It is important for Sam to experience these things. Dying with Dignity is a good cause," he says.

"That's beside the point. Fourteen-year-olds do not need to experience *that*," says Mom pointing at the screen.

The clip has cut from the woman at the mic to the protest-ers shouting into the crowd.

"What started out as a peaceful rally turned quickly when a group of protesters arrived at Province House."

I'm back on the screen again, trying to get people to move aside. My arms are flailing. Suddenly I'm one of the shouters. Mom is glued to the TV. I close my eyes. I've got nothing.

CHAPTER 9

"TWICE IN A LITTLE OVER A WEEK. YOU'RE BREAKING records," says Ms. Sandford, gesturing for me to have a seat.

She was the one who wanted to see me. I'm not an idiot. This is about me skipping school the other day. So much for covering things up. It's all everyone's talking about. Guys walk past and tap me on the shoulder, people I'm not even friends with. I'm like this hero to them. Not for supporting Dying with Dignity, but for skipping school, having my face on TV, maybe them thinking I got away with it.

"I understand you've been pretty busy," she says, sending me a serious look.

May as well own it, take whatever punishment I've got coming to me. If only I hadn't been nabbed by that reporter.

I shrug. "I skipped and got busted. What's there to say?"

"Indeed, you did. Even made your TV debut. I'm impressed," she says, raising an eyebrow. She folds her hands on top of her desk.

"Dad forgot to email." And after seeing my face on TV last night, I forgot to remind him. My one mistake. All I needed was for Dad to confirm that he was aware of my absence. But then, it only makes sense that someone from school would have seen me on TV.

"I'm not sure attending a rally is a good excuse for missing school," she says. "It could send a message to the other

47

students—that it's okay to take a day off if you think you have a good reason? That could leave the door wide open to interpretation. Believe me, there would be kids coming up with lots of these good reasons."

"But Dad knows..."

She sends me a look that tells me not to butt in while she's talking. "I've spoken to Mr. Feener."

I shift in my chair. Of course she has.

"We agreed that given your situation at home, an afterschool detention might not be for the best. We know your mother depends on you to help out and we don't want to add to that burden for her."

Special treatment. Not that I want to stay after school. If I was another kid I could be facing a two-day suspension.

"That said, we feel there needs to be some sort of disciplinary action taken. We don't want this setting a precedent." She pauses. "Does that make sense to you?"

I nod. The rally was important. But she's right. Besides, I knew Mom wouldn't want me to go.

"I've given this some thought, and here's what I've decided. You are temporarily suspended—"

"Suspended!"

She puts up her hand. "Let me finish. You're temporarily suspended from submitting any blog posts for a month."

"A month? But the post. You said I could write it." She knows what writing that post means to me. It's personal this time. Not only that, in a month I could write a dozen more.

"You're not listening, Sam. I didn't say you couldn't write it. I said it can't be submitted for a month. There's a difference."

I've been planning it in my head, deciding what to write. I know it's no good to complain, but still. This sucks.

"Off the record, your parents should be proud to have a son who stands up for what he believes in," she adds.

A lot of good that does me. I don't tell her Mom was pretty pissed when she found out I'd skipped school to attend the rally, or that she accused Dad of keeping secrets from her. Mom did cave after she saw me standing up to the protesters. She got a little teary-eyed. "You're too much like your dad," she said, then made me promise not to skip school again or I'd be grounded. I wasn't sure how that would work, since these days I haven't got a social life. In the end it was all good. We managed to smooth things out. This punishment of Sandford's is going to hurt.

The conversation shifts. Next thing I know, she brings up my writing. Nice touch, considering the punishment she just gave me. Sandford pulls a small navy-blue notebook from her desk drawer and slaps it down in front of me.

I shake my head, confused. "What's that?"

Ms. Sandford smiles.

Okay, so I sound clueless. "I know what it *is*, but what's it for?" I say.

"Take it with you and write things down as they happen. Use it to keep track of what's going on—thoughts, feelings, reminders, memories."

"A diary?" Of all the ridiculous suggestions. I give her a look and she raises her eyebrow in return.

"Think of it as a pocket notebook," she says.

"I'm not keeping a diary." All I need is for the guys to find *that* out. They already think I'm a loser for giving up hockey.

She goes right on talking. "Do you know cursive?"

"Well, yeah, but..." Two years ago, Mrs. Keating offered to teach anyone who was interested in learning. Mom and Dad made sure I was one of them.

"Excellent. Cursive will allow the words to flow onto the paper. It'll be faster and easier to jot things down as they come to you." I wait to see what else she has to say, but that seems to be about it. "Then you're all set."

"I already said, I'm not writing in a diary." What's it going to take to get through to her?

"A lot of famous people carried pocket notebooks. Mark Twain...Darwin."

Seriously, does she think I'm going to jump right on this? I'm not that needy. "No offense, but they're both boring." Who cares about a bunch of old guys from forever ago?

"How about George Lucas?"

"Lucas? Please."

"Hemingway?"

I shift positions.

She tilts her head. "So—I finally have your attention."

I stay quiet.

"You have a bit in common with him, actually. He started writing in high school, too. Did you know that?"

"Yeah, and won a Pulitzer *and* Nobel Prize for literature. But probably not because of a pocket diary."

"I see you've done your homework."

I shrug. We read *The Old Man and the Sea* in Gerrard's class a few weeks back. Hemingway's pretty cool.

"All the more reason for you to take the notebook."

I try to stop her in her tracks. This isn't going to go the way she thinks it will.

"Didn't he die by suicide?"

Again, she looks impressed. "Yes, he did. But it would be a mistake to let his death overshadow all the wonderful stories he wrote when he was living. People should be remembered for what they did, not how they died."

Did she manipulate this whole conversation just so she could make that point? Maybe she's even tougher than I thought.

"You don't yet look convinced. Believe me, writing out what you're going through can make a big difference to how you cope with it."

The sun shines in through the window behind Sandford, making her purple hair look even weirder than it actually is. Standing, she smiles and nudges the notebook toward me like it's all settled.

"Just give it a try. It'll be helpful. I promise. One day you'll be glad you did. You're a gifted writer."

"Keeping a diary isn't *writing*." I'm not a little kid who'll do whatever she wants just because she says something nice to me. And if she was really interested in my writing, she wouldn't have suspended me from writing for the blog. There's a lot of messed-up thoughts in my head these days, and I do mean a lot, well beyond the things I write about for the blog—teen suicide, poverty, school lunch programs, bullying, environmental issues, body image, that sort of thing. Gets a lot of the garbage off my chest, so I guess in that sense the blog-writing is therapeutic. Except the things I write about don't cut too close to *my* surface. I make sure of that. All that was about to change until this suspension. I think about the proposal I sent Jim. No blog posts for a month. He's not going to be happy. Traffic to the site has gone bonkers since I started writing for it.

"Writing is writing, Sam, whether it's the school blog or a personal journal. You have a passion for causes. It's in every article you write."

"I thought this was a pocket notebook."

Sandford gives me that weird look again. "You know what's important to you," she adds, like she has me figured out. Impossible. Even I don't have me figured out.

"You mean lost causes?" I laugh sarcastically.

"You fight for justice, Sam. That tells me a lot about you as a person. Not only that, you get people thinking and talking. That's how we make change in the world. We find a cause and bring others on board." She's starting to sound like Dad, and I know there's something to what she's saying. But I'm still not falling for this whole "pocket notebook" idea of hers.

"I'm not keeping a diary. That's too nerdy," I tell her, folding my arms across my chest. "You calling it a journal doesn't change anything. I'm smarter than that." I'm not holding anything back. Ms. Sandford tells us to say it like it is, but say it with respect.

"Suit yourself," she says finally, putting the notebook away.

———

I don't bother going to the cafeteria for lunch. Instead, I climb the bleachers out behind the ballfield. There's one other person sitting in the stands. I can't tell who it is from this distance. I unzip my backpack, take out my pen and black notebook, and start writing.

Sandford's cool, a bit old school. I have more in common with Hemingway than I thought. Writers carrying notebooks—a no-brainer. Have been avoiding Noah and the guys. Feels easier that way. Maybe I am a nerd.

I snap the notebook shut and put it away. I look across the bleachers. Someone has joined the mystery person. I thought they were a loner, like me. Guess I was wrong. I don't like that

I misled Sandford. I just don't want her knowing everything about me. I should have been honest, told her I already have a notebook. Except the notebook is private, meant only for me. It would feel weird if she knew.

The bell rings. I grab my backpack and head off to class.

CHAPTER 10

"SO NICE TO SEE YOU, NOAH." MOM MAKES A SMALL, satisfied noise as she leans across the counter toward us. "Feels just like old times. Doesn't it, Sam?"

She's wrong. Nothing about this feels like old times. Noah hasn't been over since I dropped out of hockey. And I can't even remember the last time he invited me to his place. We used to be inseparable.

"Nice seeing you too, Mrs. Gillis," he says, wiping his mouth on his shoulder. "Mom says hi. She's been planning to call." He looks like he's searching for something more to say. He shrugs and sends Mom a feeble look. "At least, that's what she keeps saying." That's a load of crap. His mother hasn't called Mom in ages and I'm pretty sure she doesn't plan to. We're officially the family that makes other people uncomfortable.

I get why Mom's so happy to see Noah. I just wish she'd bring it down a notch. She worries about my nonexistent social life.

"You're fourteen. You should be out having fun with your friends," she said the other day. But most fourteen-year-olds don't have a life like this. It's complicated and messy and scary too.

I bite into my Pizza Pocket, hoping Mom doesn't overdo it with her show of gratitude at Noah being here.

Mom keeps watching me and Noah like she can't believe he's here sitting at the kitchen counter with me, chowing down on Pizza Pockets and Coke. A part of me can't believe it either. Her hair's done up in a sloppy bun—her casual at-home look. These days she only wears makeup when she goes out with friends, which isn't all that often. Not like back in the day when she was an admin at Dalhousie University and planned fund-raising events in her spare time. Mom's a planner. It's what she does best. Not that she doesn't make plans now, it's just done on a much smaller scale.

There's tomato sauce on Noah's chin and in the corners of his mouth. I don't bother telling him. Pizza Pockets are messy, but then so is Noah. Grabbing a napkin, I wipe the corners of my own mouth, just in case. Mom leans farther across the counter, like a vulture waiting for its next meal.

"It's been too long since you've been over, Noah. I'm so glad to see you boys hanging out together." Nice going, Mom. No one said things were back to the way they were. This could be a one-time thing. I mean, hockey's gone. Noah's playing in tournaments while I'm home every weekend playing Xbox and helping with Dad. Things just aren't the same between us.

Noah looks up at Mom mid-chomp and gives an awkward smile. He reaches for his soda, tips it up, and swallows hard. I wait for the belch that doesn't come. Guess he's holding back because Mom's in the room.

I sure hope Mom doesn't start getting sentimental. She has this way of embarrassing me in front of my friends. With me being an only kid, she doesn't get as much practice being a parent as other moms, and it shows.

"Do you remember the time you boys tried sleeping out in the tent out back?" Great. Here we go down memory lane. I polish off my food, anxious to get away.

Noah smiles into his Pizza Pocket. He looks up at Mom and grins. "I still say that was a bear we heard." Reaching for a napkin this time, he finally wipes the sauce from his mouth. He gives a small laugh, remembering. The story's not funny the way it used to be. We laughed about it for weeks afterward. Now it only gets a small chuckle.

Mom's beaming. For her, this means something. I don't know what—maybe that Noah's still a part of my world. I mean, I'd probably still hang out with him, I just don't know what we'll talk about. My interests have changed. Noah doesn't get the writing thing. After my first blog entry, he laughed and said, "Sounds like you've got a thing for Jessica Pearce." When more blog posts followed, he kept quiet, but only because he's my best friend.

I'm pretty sure he doesn't want to hear about all the up-to-date technology and research being done with ALS either. Doing the Ice Bucket Challenge was one thing, but Noah's not going to make ALS his life, not the way I have—I get that.

It's clear that Mom would like to have *normal* back. The tent story happened when we were about nine. We were all psyched to spend the night outdoors. It was early May. Mom said it was too cold to sleep outside, that we'd end up coming into the house in the middle of the night. I told her no way, we were spending the whole night and that was that. Only, Noah woke up to some strange noises in the bushes outside the tent. I blasted him for waking me up from a dead sleep. My guess is it was a family of raccoons. I couldn't convince Noah. He ran for the house, screaming like he was being chased by zombies. Thanks to Noah, we ended up camped out on the living room floor in our sleeping bags, Rosie lying between us, snoring like an old man in a nursing home.

Noah puts the stained napkin on his plate, takes a chug from his Coke. Mom's still staring. If she gets misty-eyed, I'm out of here. I get it—it's been a while since I've hung out with Noah. But does she have to draw attention to it?

I suggest we go play some Xbox in my room. Noah's eyes light up when I tell him I've got *Dying Light*.

He shrugs and says, "Cool," but I know Noah. He's super excited. If you want to get Noah's attention, mention hockey or zombies. Those two things get him every time. Add in the fact that *Dying Light* has only been out a few weeks and he's in zombie heaven. We head off to my room. Mom trails behind us. If she goes up to my room to watch us play, I'll never live it down. I'm not five years old, Mom.

"Why don't you stay over tonight, Noah? I could call your mom."

What the...? She doesn't even know if I'm okay with it. I look back and give her a what-do-you-think-you're-doing look, but she ignores me. She thinks she knows what's best. "It would *really* be like old times then—wouldn't it, Sam?" she says, flashing me a big smile.

Noah goes to say something, but then the door to Dad's room swings open. My eyes zoom straight to the hospital bed and the lift we use for getting Dad in and out of bed.

"Make room for the boss man," says Marcie, barrelling her way out of Dad's room. She stops when she sees us in the living room. "Hey there, Noah. Long time, no see. Where have you been keeping yourself?"

Noah's face goes red and he croaks out a quick, "Hey, Marcie."

I hear Dad's wheelchair, and then he appears in the doorway. I stand there stunned. Noah hasn't seen Dad since the Ice Bucket Challenge. I shoot Noah a look. The shock registers on his face. Dad's lost weight and he sometimes has trouble keeping his mouth closed, like now.

"Good to see you, Noah," he says, then makes his way into the living room. I can tell Noah's thrown by the sound of Dad's banked voice.

Noah doesn't respond at first, just stands there with the deer-in-the-headlights-look. I get it, it's a little weird, hearing Dad speak with his mouth not moving. Took me a while too. I want to say something, but don't know what.

Marcie closes the door behind Dad. Mom hurries over like she needs to help out, but Dad doesn't need help. What's more, she knows he doesn't. She should have seen him the day of the rally, the way he made his way through the crowd.

Lately, he hasn't been into going outdoors, not the way he used to. After the rally, he started keeping a low profile. He's been spending more time in his room, even though Marcie tells him it's not good to be closed off from the rest of the world. What bothers me is what he thinks about when he's in there all alone. I'm pretty sure it's things I'd rather not know.

The other day I saw the issue of *Vanity Fair* in his room. It was open to the article about Jack Kevorkian. I remember when it came out. It was the same year Dad was diagnosed. After he died, Kevorkian made the news all over again. I was old enough to know what Mom and Dad were talking about, how Kevorkian helped people die but it wasn't legal.

I wondered why Dad was reading the article again. It wasn't like I could ask. I pretended not to see it. Wasn't sure I wanted to know his reasons.

"I finally convinced this one to take a break from his work," says Marcie to no one in particular. "The things you have to go through to get a date these days." She looks down at Dad and smiles. I stand speechless, staring at Dad's expressionless face. He's wearing that stupid hat with the wings on the sides, the one Marcie got him a few months back at a thrift store. The design on the crest says *There's No Flying Without Wings*. A pair of sunglasses rest on the beak of his cap. Definitely not something Dad would have worn three years ago. But you don't say no to

Marcie. It was all good because Dad actually thought the cap was funny. He took one look at it and said, "Right on." I wonder what his lawyer friends would say if they could see him now.

I close my eyes. Noah must think we're a freak show. I didn't expect him to see Dad like this when I invited him over. He looks as though he's seen a ghost, and in some ways he has. Dad's a ghost of himself.

My appetite for Xbox is suddenly gone. I'm pretty sure Noah doesn't want to play either. This whole afternoon has gone down the tubes. Maybe I should have warned Noah before inviting him over. It wasn't fair of me. It's just that Dad's been working pretty steady these past few weeks. He usually spends the afternoon in his room. He hasn't really talked about it, but I know it's volunteer, since he quit at the law firm. Legal Aid or more Dying with Dignity? I'm not sure. Marcie's a force when she puts her mind to it. She can usually talk him into doing things he'd rather not. But does she have to be so freaking persuasive all the time?

Noah picks his head up and looks at me. "Hey, it's been good hanging out, Sam, but I should probably take off. Nice seeing you, Mrs. Gillis. Mr. Gillis," Noah says—no, scratch that, he mumbles awkwardly, like he can't wait to get away. Mom tells him not to hurry off, but by now he's reaching for the doorknob. It's like he's speeding down the ice, heading for the net. He's already halfway out the door.

"Wait up," I say, grabbing my coat from the hallway closet. I turn back toward Dad. His eyes meet mine. The door closes. I don't even say goodbye.

CHAPTER 11

WE WALK. AT THIS POINT I'VE GOT NOTHING. CAN'T think of a single thing worth saying that would explain to Noah what he just saw.

"Sorry," he says. I shoot him a look. He shrugs and says, "I mean your dad."

"Oh, that." But why is *he* apologizing? I try to make it sound as if it's no big deal, that everyone's dad has a debilitating disease that could end his life at any time.

"Must suck. You know...knowing he won't get better." He's looking down at the sidewalk, dragging his feet. He's right. It does suck. It sucks big time, and there's nothing I can do about it. I shrug and look down at the ground, kick at some loose gravel along the way.

"Your dad was such a great guy."

We keep walking. It's hard to know what to say. Noah's right. Dad *was* a great guy, the kind of dad who never missed a game unless it absolutely couldn't be avoided. He took time off work to go to the tournaments. He was the kind of dad who would call all your buddies over for a backyard barbeque, who would listen when you had a problem. Not so he could solve it for you, but to help you figure it out on your own. Yeah, that *was* my dad.

I'm probably the one who should be apologizing to Noah. I invited him over to keep Mom off my back. That wasn't fair of me. These days I drag everyone down around me.

Noah treating me differently because my dad is going to die—I get that. The other guys don't make jokes the way they used to. They're not sure how to behave around me. I traded in my hockey stick for a keyboard. I'm not who they thought I was.

Maybe the only thing keeping my friendship with Noah together was our love of the game, us playing on the same team. At least, that's how it seems. Maybe it's all me. Maybe I'm jealous. He gets to do all the things I can't anymore. I'm not exactly sure when our friendship started going off the rails, but I do know it was long before the Ice Bucket Challenge. The challenge was a last-ditch effort to patch things up. Me dropping out of hockey was the final straw.

"Why don't we check out the mall?" I say as we walk past the skate park. It's deserted except for two kids doing flat-land tricks. They're not wearing helmets; beginners, trying to look cool, just young enough to think they'll never get hurt. They don't even know the rules. I fight the urge to tell them to go home before they're injured. I make a quick mental note: maybe there's an article here.

"So...your dad still works?" says Noah as we continue down the sidewalk. His question comes out clumsy.

"Yeah. Why wouldn't he?" What, does he think Dad's not as smart as he used to be?

Noah gives me a weird look, shrugs and says he doesn't know. "I just thought maybe..."

"Guess you thought wrong." Dad plans to keep up his work through Legal Aid until the time comes.... I've got to stop thinking that way. I change the subject. We talk about nothing much as we continue down the sidewalk. Noah jabbers on about a girl he likes, Monica. She's new at Forest Glenn this year. I've seen her around. Brown hair, amber eyes. I heard she's into soccer.

"She's cute," I tell Noah, and that seems to please him.

The breeze is cool, but the sun is nice. Great being out like this, me and Noah, just being ourselves for once. No heavy thoughts. My senses are on high alert and I'm aware of all the little things in my path—the colour of the grass, the sound of the leaves rustling, a dog barking in the distance—and I like it. If I was alone, I'd probably pull out my notebook, maybe describe how I'm feeling right now, no worries, no pressure. Free.

We decide to grab a bus and head downtown, something we used to do all the time. These days it's an anomaly. Someone shoves their way between us as we're getting ready to board the bus, Noah calls out and tells the guy to slow down. I can feel his irritation. His body language gives him away.

"Chill, man, it's okay," I say to Noah. Small things set him off sometimes.

"Jackass," Noah sputters, his muscles tense.

I put my hand on his shoulder. "Let it go, dude. It's nothing."

I hope the guy didn't hear him. Seriously, he looks like he could squish Noah between his fingers. I don't have a death wish. Noah needs to check himself before he goes off like that. He got benched during the tournament last spring. Sure, stuff gets to you when you're out on the ice, players on the other team just looking to start something, but it's not worth it. Anger's okay. It keeps you determined. Acting on that anger isn't.

Noah stares at me. He's pissed. But then his expression changes and he starts up the bus steps.

"Come on," he says looking back at me. I smile and jump onboard. The guy who pushed his way ahead of us is sitting near the middle of the bus. I looked down as we shuffle past, hoping Noah keeps his mouth shut. Can't wait to start moving.

Being on the bus with Noah feels normal; people talking, doing their own thing. No one knows my story. I look around. Smile. Not bad. I could get used to this.

———

The mall is dead—to be expected on a weekday afternoon. A bunch of seniors are sitting in front of the doughnut shop, probably complaining about the government. Noah suggests we get some fries. They taste like garbage but I load them with ketchup and force them down.

Noah talks about some of the plays he and Chuck made during the last game, the way he and I used to. I pretend to care. Sounds like he and Chuck are suddenly best friends.

Without warning, he says, "Come out for the spring session. My folks could get you to practice and all the games. It's no big deal. We did it before." He swats my arm. "It'd be like old times, Sam—the two of us out on the ice again."

Hearing the excitement in his voice, for a split second, I dare to think maybe. But then reality sinks in —tournaments all over the region, staying in hotels, eating out, the cost, leaving my dad. I think about how close the end could be and it scares me.

"It's complicated," I say, shaking my head. I wish he'd lay off about hockey. Thinking about what I'm missing out on is tough enough, but explaining it over and over makes me want to puke. Why doesn't he get how hard this is for me? Wasn't he the one running away from my ghost dad?

Besides, who's to say I'd even make the team after all that time off the ice? I lower my head. Noah makes this sound easy when it's anything but. The only way my situation will change is if Dad—

I shut my mind off, change gears. "What about Chuck?" I heard they've been sharing rides.

"Best friends first," Noah says, smiling as he gives me a fist bump. "We connect on the ice. You know that."

I smile, relieved to hear him say this.

"Chuck and me—can't even compare. What do you say?" He sounds hyped up, like he's thinking maybe this could work.

I shake my head. "All that time away from home? Come on. You've seen Dad." I dip a soggy fry into some ketchup. Tournaments take us out of province for a whole weekend. In that time, things could take a turn at home. If something happened to Dad while I was away...

"I am dead serious, man." His eyes are wide open and he's giving me his goofy grin.

"Head's not in the game. It's why I dropped out in the first place, remember?" I shove a fry in my mouth, but immediately want to spit it out. Why go over all this again? Nothing has changed. There are still too many distractions. And I can't spend what time Dad has left out on the ice. I can't. Mom needs my help. We've all made sacrifices. I grab the garbage off the table and throw it away. Noah follows.

This afternoon has me really bummed out, Noah pressuring me about hockey again. I don't say much on the bus ride home. It was okay getting away for a few hours. I don't mind admitting that, but it's time to get back to the real world. The bus slows down at our stop.

"I'm thinking of asking Monica out," Noah says as we get off the bus. "What do you think? Would she go out with a star hockey player?" There's that goofy grin of his again.

"Sure, why not?" I say. "Go for it. Life's too short, right? Don't spend your time wondering what if. You'll only end up wishing you had." He nods like it's good advice, and it is. It's advice I've heard my dad give a time or two. We go our separate ways.

As I hurry home I realize something's bothering me. I think it's been bothering me since Noah said it. Dad wasn't a great guy.

He *is* a great guy.

Hung out with Noah first time in months. It felt weird when Dad came out of his room. Went with Noah to the mall to escape. Feeling like a first-class jerk. Worst son ever.

I close my notebook and drop it in my backpack. I wonder if Hemingway's life was as messed up as mine.

CHAPTER 12

"IS EVERYTHING OKAY?" DAD SAYS AS I SETTLE IN TO watch the movie. "Is there something you want to talk about?"

"Not really." What's there to say? I acted like a jerk today and we both know it. I was embarrassed by my own dad, the illness taking over his body, the way it's changed his appearance. And I was embarrassed for myself, to have Noah see what my life is like now. The real reason I gave up on hockey *and* our friendship. None of this is Dad's fault. Feels like I can't do anything right. It's this stupid disease.

"Anything I can help you with?"

I shrug and plop down into the armchair. "Just having an off day, I guess. No big deal."

"Sorry about what happened," Dad says after a moment of silence. Him saying that makes me feel like even more of a jerk than I already am.

"No problem," I say, looking toward the kitchen. Wish Mom would get out here. I can hear the sound of corn popping. I hate that I don't know what to say next. No way should Dad apologize for what happened this afternoon. Things were awkward with Noah, but that wasn't Dad's fault. That was on me. I'm the jerk, taking off the way I did. It's not as if Noah and I went out and had a good time.

"Jon texted earlier. I kind of forgot. We had plans to go to the mall."

"I'm here if you need to talk," says Dad.

"I hope I'm not late," says Mom hurrying her way to the couch with the popcorn. She looks from Dad to me. "What's this about you and Jon?" she says.

"Nothing. It's all cool," I tell her. "We had plans for the mall. That's where Noah and I went today."

I catch sight of the expression on her face. She lands the bowl of popcorn in my lap. I'm slightly glad for the distraction. She has to know I'm lying. Not that she'd admit to knowing. I can't remember the last time I hung out with Noah at the mall, let alone Jon. I reach in and pull out some popcorn. It feels wrong chomping away during movie night now that Dad can't. At least now with the voice banking he can make comments about the movies that don't take forever to come out.

"It was so good seeing Noah today." Mom's still beaming from this afternoon. Wish she'd get it out of her head that everything's back to normal between Noah and me.

"I probably should have said he was coming over, but it was kind of last minute." Another lie. We made plans two days ago. I ran into him at the school cafeteria and I didn't know what to say. It was the first thing that came flying out of my mouth. I wouldn't have invited him, but Mom had been bugging me about it. Why didn't I give her fair warning? I should have known Noah suddenly showing up at the house like that would throw her off. These days, she doesn't like spur of the moment. She likes plans—solid, well-made plans.

Dad might have stayed in his room. Guilt rips through me again.

Mom asks if I've heard how the team is doing. The way the guys are treating me like an outsider, I don't even want to think about hockey. I tell her no and quickly change the subject, start telling them both about this thing called worming that I stumbled across online, new experiments for finding a way to slow down ALS by using worms.

"Sounds cool," I tell them. "And if it can slow down the disease, it'll give us more time." I got pretty excited when I was reading the article.

Mom and Dad look at each other. She gives a soft smile.

"You need to stop this, Sam," she says. "All this researching online when you could be doing other things. Right now, there are no answers and we have to be realistic—all of us. These things you're reading about are all in the experimental stage. The reality..."

I'm shaking my head. I don't want to hear any more.

She clears her throat. "The reality is, these things are too far off in future. They aren't going to help your dad. We need to accept that. Enjoy what time we have, for as long as we have. Do you understand?"

I reluctantly nod.

She takes a deep breath. "Okay, good," she says, placing a hand on my knee. "Now let's get ready to watch the movie."

The opening credits start and I clear my throat.

"What's the movie about?" she says, settling into the sofa.

"Kind of a love story, I guess." Pushing this afternoon out of my mind, I reach into the bowl of popcorn, bring out another handful, and shove some in my mouth.

She gives me a curious look. "You picked a love story?"

Smiling, I nod. She thinks I'm talking crap. I pass her the popcorn.

"Think of it as a post-apocalyptic romance with a twist of humour," I say with my mouth full. I'm paraphrasing Roger Ebert.

"You? A romance?"

"Don't knock it," I say, trying to sound serious. Mom raises an eyebrow. A second passes and then we laugh, Dad with his voice-banked laughter. It's kind of nice knowing when something strikes him funny.

The movie starts. Nicholas Hoult looks great in his zombie role. *Warm Bodies.* I picked it because I like flicks with zombies in them. This one's different because the zombie's the main character and actually tells the story. Mom's not a fan of anything to do with the undead. She tolerates the movies I choose. She deserves props for that. But then, I'm forced to watch her corny Hallmark movies, so I guess it's a fair trade-off. Neither of us complain, because that's the whole point of movie night.

Dad will watch anything. But when it's his pick, it's usually an adventure. Planes crashing into mountains and people eating each other to survive. Fascinating in a gross way. Shows how resilient the human spirit can be when pushed to the limit. Kind of like what Dad's going through. Only in his case we know what the outcome is going to be. No way is he going to survive, regardless of how resilient his spirit is.

"It'll teach us tolerance," Dad said when movie night first became a thing in our house.

It's hard to concentrate on the movie. I keep thinking about what Mom said, about us being realistic. I know she's right. But it's still hard.

Mom passes the bowl back to me. The popcorn quickly disappears. The awkwardness from this afternoon keeps bugging me as the images come across the screen. It's hard to sit still. Unlike this afternoon, I can't just up and leave. I really *do* want to see the movie.

I stare at the TV, waiting for the story to unfold, for the zombies to appear. Waiting—seems that's all I do these days.

Later, alone in my room, I touch the pen to my notebook and write out: *Can't stop these weird thoughts going through my head, like I'm planning things out, figuring out how it will go down when/if the time comes. That's it. No more promises for me.*

CHAPTER 13

I'M SUDDENLY WIDE AWAKE. I HEAR MOM OUT IN THE living room. The TV comes on and she quickly turns down the volume. Noises are magnified at night. I hear them all. She'll fall asleep with the sound turned down low unless Dad's having another bad night. I turn over in bed. I know she's upset. I overheard her and Dad talking earlier this evening, she said he should give some more thought to getting trached and vented.

"It won't slow down the progression," he said. "And I'd be attached to a ventilator all the time. That's not for me."

I read about it online. It would require Mom to learn a whole new set of skills and Dad would need twenty-four–hour care. It would also prolong the inevitable, which has been Dad's argument against those things from the start.

It sounded like maybe she wanted him to agree to it, but I know Mom. She'll respect his wishes. She won't try and talk him into it. Awhile back he agreed to using a BiPAP machine at night to help with his breathing. I read that people with ALS on BiPAP live a bit longer.

Impossible to sleep. Too much on my brain, my running off today with Noah, lying about it. I get up and sit at my computer. I glance down at the framed photo of me and Rosie. Dad took it the year we went to camp with him. Smiling, I pick it up. Life sure was simpler back then. Thinking it would be great to go back to those simpler times, I set the photo down and start working on the blog post I won't get to submit for a whole month.

STILL A GREAT DAD

BY SAM GILLIS

I never asked to be the kid whose dad is going to die soon, but I am. My dad has ALS, so it's inevitable. ALS is a progressive disease that is slowly paralyzing my dad, even though his brain function is normal. He can't walk or talk anymore. Eventually he won't be able to eat, swallow, or breathe, but he is just as smart as he was before ALS. Most people reading this already know that about him. The doctor said my dad probably has two to five years to live. That was three years ago.

Because of that, people treat me differently and I don't want them to. Things have changed for me these past few years, but I'm still a normal teen, only now I'm trying to make a difference in the world, to honour my dad who has done plenty to help people all his life. It's partly why I did the Ice Bucket Challenge last summer: to raise awareness and money. But there's a face to ALS, not just numbers and statistics. Real people living with the disease and those who've been touched by it. I'm one of them.

The oldest living person with ALS is Stephen Hawking. Most people on the planet have heard of him. In case you haven't, he's a physicist and an author. He's won tons of awards for his work. A voice synthesizer helps him speak. He's in a wheelchair and has been living with ALS since 1963. He was twenty-one when he was first diagnosed. That's just seven years older than me.

Like Stephen Hawking, my dad does good work. He makes a difference in the world. He fights for justice. He's not famous, like Stephen Hawking. After he's gone, he won't be remembered for long, except by my mom and me. He won't receive any awards for his work. But people knowing or not knowing about him won't change the good he did. My dad uses his influence as a lawyer to help get petitions up and signed. He fights for affordable housing and for people who can't afford to pay a lawyer, no matter who they are. That will be his legacy.

These days, my dad is all about MAD—Medically Assisted Death. He wants to die with dignity when the time comes and if he's just too tired to keep going. He says that people have a right to say what their end of life will look like. Why should that be left up to someone else to decide? No one should have to suffer for the rest of their life. You might agree that for someone who's not going to get better, it is cruel to let them suffer. But not everyone thinks that way.

Two bills on doctor-assisted death have been introduced in parliament. There are people in government who agree with the Right to Die movement, and it might get passed one day, but it will be too late for my dad. Bills can take years to become law while government makes up its mind. This is nothing new.

Lawmakers have been fighting about doctor-assisted death for a long time.

Since my dad's diagnosis, the name Jack Kevorkian has been talked about in my house. In the 1990s Kevorkian built a death machine. In total, he helped 130 terminally ill people end their lives. Because of it, people called him Dr. Death. He was sent him to prison for eight years.

In all likelihood, my dad will not be here when MAD becomes law. He will either die from ALS or else break the law and have someone like Jack Kevorkian assist him.

Before he got sick, my dad came to all my hockey games. He encouraged me to always do my best. He told me to find a way to help others. He was a great dad. He is still a great dad. Not even ALS can take that away from him or from me. He might not be able to attend hockey games anymore but he is still the same guy on the inside, where it really counts.

As for MAD, no one should have to break the law to end their suffering and pain—at least in my opinion.

——

The post stirs up a lot of crud for me that I wasn't expecting. Will I have the guts to hit send when the time comes? All the things I've been trying to keep private. Everyone will know. Or will I go back and make changes to the post before the month is up?

I don't hear the TV. Maybe Mom's finally asleep. I turn off my computer and go back to bed, ordering my brain to shut down too. Only it won't listen. I'm stuck in bed thinking back to when this all started.

Dad's voice sounded hollow, coming from inside his office. The seriousness of his tone made me stop and listen. He was talking to Mom

I'd been hanging out with Noah but we got bored playing Xbox. I decided to come home and do some surfing online. A week before, they'd told me about Dad's ALS and it still hadn't sunk in, how it would all affect me. I started researching it to find out what I could. A lot of it, I didn't understand.

"Things could get messy, Dee. This disease is so unpredictable. I want to make sure I've covered all my bases. I don't want Sam to go through what I did with Dad. He's just a kid."

"You've read too much about Kevorkian," said Mom. "Look at that farmer in Alberta. They put him away for ten years. Do you know what that would do to Sam...if he lost us both?"

"It won't come to that," said Dad.

"You think what Kevorkian did was good, and I'm not saying it wasn't, but it also wasn't legal. What you're suggesting isn't either. That's not like you."

"It's not legal yet, but it will be," said Dad. "Maybe not in my lifetime. That's why I need to be prepared. In case I reach the tipping point."

"We've talked all this over in past. I agree with you, in theory. I don't think I can be the one, Gregory," said Mom. She was troubled. I could hear it in her voice.

"There's no one else I trust."

Mom might have been crying. I couldn't tell.

"Okay?" said Dad. He paused then kept on talking. "I could order a package online. They come with simple instructions. It would look natural, that I just stopped breathing. You'd have to get rid of the evidence."

"I don't know, Greg." I leaned against the wall. I could hardly catch my breath, my heart was going crazy.

"It would be close to the end, Dee. Don't look sad," he said. "I'm not ready to opt out just yet. I've got too much work ahead of me." He gave a small laugh then quietly said, "Promise me you'll at least think about it."

I knew this was serious stuff. I couldn't believe Dad was asking Mom to break the law. But what if he was suffering and just couldn't take it? That wouldn't be fair to him. I raced off to my room, making a silent promise to do what Dad wants if the time comes and Mom can't.

CHAPTER 14

THE PROMISE I MADE TO MYSELF THREE YEARS AGO is following me. I try to shake it, but I can't get it out of my head. I had no idea how hard it would actually be when it came right down to it.

The package Dad and Mom were talking about three years ago was sitting on the counter the other day when I got home from school. I knew right away what it was. But it's only October. I wasn't expecting the package to show up for months, maybe even a year from now. Maybe never.

Mom was in the living room with Marcie. She was crying.

"You'll get through this," Marcie was saying, while rubbing Mom's back. I'm not used to seeing Mom so sad. She's usually upbeat.

Since then, it's all I've been thinking about. Clearly, Mom won't be able to help Dad. It's up to me. A promise is a promise. I can't back out now. Dad needs me.

And now, there are only two ways out of this—be the good son or the not-so-good son. My choice. But which one can I live with?

It's Saturday morning and Mom's in town. I'm here alone with Dad, a bundle of nerves. Not a good place to be.

I close my notebook and head to Dad's room. I stand outside, shut my eyes for a few seconds before going in. I've got this. It's not like I didn't know this day was coming. I can't wiggle into the past and alter my destiny. Some things you can change; this promise isn't one of them. It's too important to Dad. Over time, I've learned to be realistic. Don't sugarcoat the facts, because the facts won't sugarcoat you.

Mom got Dad ready for the day, but after breakfast he wanted to rest. I look over at him asleep in his hospital bed. I'm pretty sure Mom put the kit in his closet. I reach for the shelf but then freeze, pulling my hand back. I take a deep breath. It's no good to keep putting this off. I know that. The parcel sitting on the counter the other day, Mom crying in the living room, I knew what it all meant. She couldn't do it. She couldn't do what Dad wants. What he's said all along that he wants. Now it's up to me.

Reaching onto the shelf again, I look past Dad's neatly stacked collection of board games, his books on dying with dignity, and then I hit upon the package. I stand there holding it like it's about to explode in my hands.

Seems that I should say something to Dad, but I don't know what that something should be. They say actions speak louder than words. Maybe that's true. I'm not sure. I'm about to cross this line; there'll be no going back. That's the one thing I am sure of. I've played it out in my mind like a trillion times, imagined both worst and best-case scenarios. Feels as though I should be ready for anything that comes up.

But, here's the thing.

I'm really not ready at all.

I read through the instructions. They are pretty straight-forward. Rereading and rereading and rereading them won't make any difference. I set the paper aside and get on with it. No reason to hurry. Mom won't be back for an hour, and according to the instructions this will only take minutes.

I look at Dad. He's awake. There's this look in his eyes; he can't believe what I'm about to do. A part of me doesn't believe it either. I swallow and squeeze the package in my hands. The fingers on his right hand move, his eyes dart toward the SGD that is out of his reach. He wants to say goodbye, but I don't want to hear. I can't. This is hard enough without hearing him say goodbye.

My hands tremble and Dad sees it. His mouth opens a tiny bit, then closes. Nothing comes out. He speaks through his eyes now. I once thought I always knew what he wanted to say. These days I'm not sure. His own words are gone. He doesn't even gurgle.

I shake out the nerves and keep going. Some drool runs out the corner of his mouth. He'd wipe it away if he could move his hand that far. He cared a lot about his appearance. Ties and socks always matched—a family joke that Dad used to pretend he minded. Shirts expertly pressed when he went to the office. (He ironed them himself.) His hair was always combed and neat. He was handsome—but he's not anymore. And I'm not saying that to be mean. It's just how it is. I look over at Dad lying in bed. So much has changed in three years.

And just so you know, there was never any drool before.

The tissues are on the nightstand beside the bed. Before I can pull one from the box, I stop. This is Mom's job, but she's not here. She's in town, having coffee with the faithful three. I take the Saturday morning shift for her. Marcie comes to the house to help out for six or seven hours every other day, although she's flexible on those days. Saturday is her day off to spend time with Olivia. It's non-negotiable. Aunt Tess drops in on Thursday evenings. Rupert comes by from time to time. He sits with Dad and looks out the window. He was friends with Grandpa Gillis about a hundred years ago. He's known Dad since he was a kid. I wonder what's it's like for Rupert, knowing that even though he's ancient, he's probably going to outlast someone he's known since they were a little kid.

Last week Marcie told Mom it was time she hired more help.

"Gregory doesn't like strangers." That is always Mom's excuse.

"Well, he got used to me, didn't he?" said Marcie. She wasn't backing down. "Sometimes you've got to be okay with things you're not okay with."

Seriously, I think Mom is the one who doesn't want strangers coming in.

Last night during dinner, Mom announced that she was hiring more help. "I'll post an ad," she said. For the first time, she didn't ask Dad if he was okay with it.

I look down at Dad.

More drool.

Like a flowing river, it's about to drip onto the clean white sheets.

"No drool, remember?" I say, shaking my head. It was something we agreed upon ahead of time—I was to feel no guilt for living my own life, offer no apologies, and wipe no drool. Wish now I'd added *no ending life* to that. Right now, I'd trade in all those other things to put it on the list. But it's too late for that.

Back when we wrote all this down, we were able to laugh a little. Dad said finding the humour in a situation keeps you in a better frame of mind. I try to think of one of Dad's jokes, but other than the no diaper reference, I'm drawing a blank. There's nothing about my present situation that seems the least bit funny. Sorry, Dad.

I look to see some recognition in Dad's eyes. I hope he remembers the things he decided on beforehand. I shake my head; of course he remembers. It's not like his mind is gone.

It's just trapped inside a body that's dying a bit every day. What's wrong with me?

"I'm doing what you want," I say as Dad continues to look up at me. My hands are fumbling. "I heard you and Mom. I know she can't do it, so I'm helping."

I remember my dad saying, "Don't worry. It will look natural. I've read up on it, Dee. No one will know."

"But what if you can't communicate? How will I know you're ready?" said Mom.

When the time comes, you'll know. His answer to Mom that day, the one I've heard so many times, echoes in my mind now. The kit showing up at the house the other day, it was Dad's way of telling her the time was right.

I move toward Dad, my heart filling my chest and throat. I look into his eyes. No one will know. No one but you and me.

I lean in closer. He's blinking. A tear forms in the corner of his eye.

But then reality hits me.

I can't do this. What was I thinking?

I step back, shaking my head. Take a deep breath in.

Dad's eyes are glazed and soft. He's telling me it's okay, he understands. I pull back, ashamed.

What am I any good for? I want to yell. My throat tightens and my head starts spinning. The room feels like it's about to collapse in on me. I look at the kit I'm squeezing. My hands are trembling. This feels all wrong. I've got to get out of here. Fast.

CHAPTER 15

RACING TO MY ROOM, I START GRABBING THINGS.
Underwear, socks, a Nirvana T-shirt, an extra pair of jeans. I
rummage through my drawers, put what will fit into my backpack, and grab my iPod. Catching sight of the framed photo
of me and Rosie, I pause.

The camp. That's it! No one will think to look for me there.
The small wooden box with Rosie's name on it goes into my
backpack along with the framed photo.

I check the cost for a one-way ticket online. I still have some
money left on the pre-paid Visa I got from Mom last month. She
said fourteen meant new responsibilities when she handed me
the card, but I'm pretty sure it was just Mom trying to make up
for my quitting hockey. If the past three years haven't given me
plenty of opportunities to prove I'm responsible, then I don't
know what would. But I didn't argue her choice of words. I took
the card and promised to spend it wisely, then ordered a bunch
of dumb stuff off Amazon.

The card has a balance of $2.78 after buying the ticket. I put
it in my jacket pocket. There's probably not much point, but you
never know. I print off the ticket, fold it in two, and put it safely
in my backpack. I remember, then, there's cash in my underwear drawer, money for a video game I've been saving up for.

I count it—twenty-five bucks plus some loose change. I
shove it in my jacket pocket along with the Visa and zip it tight.
Not much, but it'll be enough. I'll make it be enough.

Seeing some M&Ms on the kitchen counter, I snap them up and put them in my pocket for a quick boost if I need one. Go to the cupboard, open my backpack, and stuff in a half-eaten bag of cookies. I'm on autopilot. My brain is barely registering. It's like I'm standing back watching myself going through the motions.

I turn toward the fridge, see the green sleeve that holds the Do Not Resuscitate form Dad placed there early on. Instructions to never put him on life support. I think about the look on Mom's face that day.

I check the time. I've got to get moving. Mom will be home soon. I leave my cellphone on the counter and head out the door. Stop suddenly. Reverse course, remembering my journal. I race to my room, pull it out from under my mattress, and slip it into my backpack. On the way out, I catch sight of my phone. Mom will worry when she sees it, but I can't chance her finding me. I'll leave a quick note. Grabbing Mom's notepad, I pause. I haven't got time to think. I start writing.

Dear Dad,

I thought I was man enough to do this, but I'm not. I hope you'll understand. I'm sorry.

Sam

Placing the note on the counter next to my cellphone, I scan the kitchen before taking off, hoping I got everything.

I step outside and look toward the late morning sky. The sun shines hot against my face. My backpack weighs against me. It feels good in an odd way. I wasn't sure I'd ever get to this point. A lot of times I hoped I wouldn't. Now here I am.

I put in my earbuds and head for the bus stop. I've got to get going if I want to make connections. The bus out of town leaves in less than an hour.

Sorry, Mom, I don't want you to worry. You'll just have to trust that I'm going to be okay.

———

The bus won't take me as far I want to go. No one's been to the ends of the earth and lived to tell about it—at least not that I've heard. But it's not as if there are a lot of options for me. The bus driver is taking people's tickets and placing their things in the luggage compartment. He looks too old to be driving a bus. So much grey hair. Marcie says when you're fourteen, anyone over forty looks old. She's probably right, but I'd never admit it to her, not that I'm planning to ever see her again.

I step onto the bus and take a seat. Window seats are best for privacy. You can turn your back on the world, make like you're taking in the scenery, and no one cares. The bus idles along noisily, waiting for everyone to board. Pushing my face against the cool glass, I rip open the M&Ms and tip the package to my mouth. I put what's left into the front pocket of my backpack.

As I stare out the bus window, I hope one day Mom will understand. My gut says she won't. I know Mom. It would be impossible to make her understand any of it. The way I failed at being the good son, the son she and Dad needed me to be. Wish I could get all of this out of my head. Things are so messed up right now. I can't think straight.

The bus fills with people, some pushing, some taking their time, some knocking their bags into the seats in front of them. They make their way down the narrow aisle as the bus engine continues to rumble. I put in my earbuds and select "Smells Like Teen Spirit." Create a whole new world for myself inside the vibrations of the music and the bus motor. A safe place where no one expects me to be anything outside the music. The song is ancient but some songs are timeless. And there are days when you need to hear Nirvana.

An old woman with a navy blue carry-on bag stops waddling past and looks down at the empty seat beside me. I'm in no mood to have someone invade my space, especially some old lady with prune skin. A bright red shiny purse with thin white cracks swings from her left arm. Looks like something straight out of the eighties, maybe even as far back as the seventies. There's a weird stain across her T-shirt that's stretched and baggy around the neck. If she zipped up her jacket no one would see.

"Hi, sonny boy," she says leaning down toward me.

I push myself down farther into the vinyl. Too late to take an aisle seat. Turning up the volume on my iPod, I want to forget this whole day. These past three years, if I were given a choice. Stop being who I am and start being who I was. But there's no going back. The Sam Gillis everyone knows no longer exists, except they don't even see it; not Mom or Dad, and for sure not Noah.

The driver shifts gears and the bus starts moving.

At the moment, I might be trapped in this seat, but a part of me still feels lighter, as I leave everything behind me. Eventually people reach their limit. I want to move ahead, start over. Ms. Sandford was right about caregivers needing a break, but I always thought that meant Mom, not me. I was wrong.

CHAPTER 16

ROSIE'S WET NOSE EXPLORES THE INSIDE OF MY EAR. Seconds later her tongue leaves a layer of slobber on the side of my face. Time for me to get up. Lights are on out in the hallway; someone's awake already. I roll over, grab Rosie by the front legs, and haul her into bed beside me. Saturday morning hockey practice, but I don't want to leave the warmth of my bed. It's still dark out. Head on my pillow, Rosie lies there looking into my eyes. Seconds later, her muscles are straining, eager to be on the move. She can't stay still.

Pots and pans are rattling in the kitchen. The smell of bacon drifts up the hallway to my room. Eggs are spitting in the frying pan. Dad's singing an old Beach Boys song. He stops and calls out, "Up and at 'em!" I sit up in bed and croak out Dad's name because I can't believe it—any of this. Rosie's breathing on me like even she knows this can't be right.

Opening my eyes, I jump, now fully awake, see what's going on, and pull back fast, cracking my head against the window. It's not Rosie at all, but that woman sitting beside me, breathing. She's leaning toward me. There's no sound coming from my iPod. The battery must have died, which sucks, because I won't have any place to recharge.

"You asleep?" she grunts. Some people can't stand not talking. She doesn't offer her hand when she says, "I'm Jody... Jody Puffin."

We pass some huge rocks along the highway. There are words spray painted on the flat surfaces: *Life—Just Live It*. It feels like a message meant for me.

When the bus stops in Chester a handful of people get off. Before she gets down her navy-blue bag, Jody asks me if I have a name—like it matters at this point.

"Jack," I tell her. "My name's Jack."

"You got a last name to go with that?"

"Kevorkian" slips out like it's no big deal.

"Well nice meeting you, Jack Kevorkian," she says. She swings her bag around and it catches the seat in front of her, but she pushes on through.

The day after he came home from the hospital with the feeding tube that would give him his meds, Dad looked at Mom and said, "I may need a Kevorkian." She gave him a look as if telling him not to say anything in front of me. Like I haven't overheard most of their conversations since Dad got sick.

Anyway, I had recently stumbled across an article Dad posted to his blog a few years back. In the article, Dad wrote about the death machine Kevorkian built back in the 1990s and his own feelings on euthanasia, and right-to-die legislation that he said would eventually become law. He has some strong feelings about what he called *the needless suffering of people who are going to eventually die from their disease.* The article ended with: *Kevorkian was a man far ahead of his time. He helped people out of their pain.*

Most people in the comment section agreed with what he had to say. But there was one comment posted by someone calling themselves *Buttercup*, ironically the name Dad would jokingly call Mom.

What if Kevorkian just liked killing people?

A lot of people fought against Jack Kevorkian's ideas. That didn't stop him from doing what he thought was right. Maybe one day that'll be me—a guy who does right no matter what people think. Right now, I feel like a failure. And using Kevorkian's name just now? What a joke. I couldn't even help my own dad. I look out to see Jody hurrying toward a parked car. She opens the door, tosses her bag in, and climbs into the passenger's side. I dig into the front pocket of my backpack, pull out my notebook, and write:

You can tell a stranger anything and it really doesn't matter. In the end they won't care if it's a lie or the truth. It just makes you anonymous.

I put my pen and notebook away and zip the pocket shut.

The one thing Kevorkian did do, he got a lot of people talking. That was back in the nineties and they're *still* debating this whole thing. I spent nights wondering what it would feel like to be known as Dr. Death for the rest of your days. Would it be worth it, to have people hate you, even if you were doing good?

CHAPTER 17

I GET OFF THE BUS AT EXIT 12 AND HEAD INTO THE Big Stop. The guy at the counter has greasy brown hair and needs a shave. I look at his name tag—*Eric*. He eyes me like he's expecting I might lift something right out from under his nose. I'm surprised there are no signs instructing people to leave their backpacks by the door.

I grab two bags of chips from the rack but put them back. There's no room for chips. They'll get crushed. Instead, I take some trail mix and debate whether to choose the bottled water or pop before pulling the water from the cooler. Eric's eyes are burning holes in the back of my head. I make my way to the counter, taking my time. I don't want to hurry. That will make it look like I've got something to hide. There's beef jerky on a rack next to the cash register. Good, but expensive. I grab some before setting it all down on the counter. This should keep me going for a while. I reach into my pocket and take out a twenty. Dude keeps watching me like a hawk. The silence between us feels weird. Taking the initiative, I start up a conversation.

"Which way to Springfield?" I ask as he scans the items. The joke Dad and I used to share whenever Springfield was mentioned suddenly pops into my head: "I'm going to visit the Simpsons. Homer and Marge are expecting me for dinner." I give Eric a goofy smile. He tells me the total but doesn't answer my question. Talk about awkward. Wish I could take my joke back. Granted, he's probably heard it a hundred times. But a smile right about now wouldn't hurt him. Customer service, dude.

He gives me back the change and I shove it in my pocket. Some people come through the door, releasing the tension. He puts my food in a bag and passes it to me. I take out the water and stuff the bag into my backpack. Dude finally gives me the directions I asked for. I mumble a quick thanks and head out the door.

Outside, I open the water and take a sip. My throat is dry and the water feels good. I put it in my already overstuffed backpack and look out at the road, at the cars speeding past. Dad made it to British Columbia back in the late eighties; surely I can make it to Springfield and Lenny's old hunting camp. My sense of direction is scrambled. I try to remember what the dude behind the counter told me. I should have paid closer attention.

I nodded like I knew exactly what he was saying but I didn't have a clue. I didn't want to seem dense, not that I care what greasy-haired Eric thinks. I remember then he said to turn right. From there it's a blur. I wonder what time it is. I could go back inside and ask, but I don't have the energy to face Eric.

I look up at the sky, searching for the direction of the sun, the way Grandpa Gillis used to do. Maybe leaving my phone behind was a mistake. Except I had no choice. I left it beside the note, so that Mom would see it and know I'd left it behind on purpose. Didn't want her freaking out, thinking I'd forgotten it, although I'm pretty sure she's freaking out right about now anyway. She's back from town and probably trying to make sense of what went on. I shouldn't have left Dad alone, even for a short time. What if he needed something? Shit. The kit. I didn't put it away. Great. Just great.

I've got to stop this, get a grip, think clearly if I expect to make it to Lenny's camp in the woods. I start walking away from the station and toward the road ahead. I pull back my shoulders. I can do this.

I stick out my thumb and walk along the shoulder of the road the way I've seen it done in movies. I smile at the drivers, hoping I look like a wholesome kid, not some troublemaking teen waiting to beat the crap out of the first person who stops to pick him up. Several cars whiz on by, pushing air at me. I continue walking. Even goodhearted people are afraid to stop for strangers. Can't really blame them. You hear things in the news.

I pick up my pace. I'll try again later.

———

Dad liked to talk about the time he hitchhiked across the country by himself. After the diagnosis came, he talked about it even more. I could tell it made him happy, a little nostalgic. It was the summer before he started university, the summer before he met Mom. He struck out on his own right after his high school graduation with a few dollars in his pocket. Grandpa and Grandma weren't happy about it. They had ideas of him working at Grandpa's law firm that summer, running errands, doing odd jobs.

Dad said he wasn't one to listen to the plans other people made for him. He'd stop off at a farm, help make hay or pick berries, anything for a few bucks, then head off again. A couple of times he even slept outdoors. He said it was peaceful at night, looking up at the sky, wondering whether there's an end to the universe or if it goes on forever.

At the time, when he told me, I thought heading off across the country like that would scare the crap out of me. And sleeping out under the stars—forget it. No way. People get killed for pocket change.

"Having only yourself to rely on brings something out in you that you never knew existed. There's not always a shoulder around to cry on, Sam, and that has to be good enough." Now I know what Dad meant when he said that.

The wind coming off the cars messes my hair, reminding me I need a haircut.

This whole situation is starting to weird me out. Do I really know what I'm doing? Can I actually make it to Lenny's camp? I suck in a breath and get a grip. If Dad made it all the way to BC, then I can find my way to a camp two hours outside of Halifax.

Cars continue to speed past. No one seems interested in some kid trying to grab a ride. My sneakers offer a decent cushion from the hard pavement. It's not long before the sun causes a trickle of sweat to run down my face. I wipe it away. It's stinking warm for late October.

Can't remember the last time I walked this far, but no one has even slowed down. I got tired of sticking my thumb out and no one offering me a ride. Depressing. Promising myself I'll try a little later, I chug down some more water and shove the bottle in my backpack where it's going to stay. All the trash and bottles I've seen on the road—disgusting. People can be pigs. Any moron knows better than to throw trash out the car window. Dad was anal about it. He kept a paper bag in the car for garbage—no exceptions. Not even a banana peel.

The road ahead reminds me that I've got no one now. I left the people in my life behind. At this point it feels as though it would take a miracle for me to reach Lenny's camp. I walk along thinking that miracles have been known to happen. You see it on the six o'clock news. People randomly reuniting, letters arriving fifty years later, someone walking away from a freak accident without a scratch or recovering from an incurable disease.

And then, like it was all planned out, the tires from a brown truck crackle across the gravel on the shoulder of the road ahead of me, slowing down. Talk about miracles; I didn't even have my thumb out. Clutching fast to my backpack, I hurry to catch up.

The truck door opens hard, could be from all the rust.

The old guy behind the wheel is wearing a red shirt with a small hole in the shoulder, and a blue ball cap with a dirty white crest that has *Shur-Gain* written on it. A dog raises its head and looks at me, then settles back down on the seat.

"Hop on in and buckle yourself up, young fella. Got no plans to pay a fine today. The driver's in control of the vehicle at all times, you know."

The roll-your-own sticking out of the old guy's mouth wags up and down when he speaks. I'm pretty sure it's just tobacco—at least I hope so. I give the dog a quick pat on the head and jump in the truck, but it doesn't react, not even when I slam the door. Tossing my backpack onto the floor, I take a deep breath. Seems too late to turn back now.

A sick feeling hits me in the gut as the seat belt locks in place. I look up and the old guy is smiling, kinda like he's a hungry lion and I'm a pork chop. He's got a few missing teeth and his day-old stubble makes him look scraggly.

Maybe this isn't such a great idea after all.

CHAPTER 18

"NICE DAY OUT THERE," THE OLD GUY SAYS, LOOKING across at me, still grinning. I don't want to sit at the side of the road chatting with a complete stranger. I wish he'd get going. I'm not looking to make a best friend or friend period, and if I was, it sure wouldn't be him.

Cars go past, turning out so they won't hit his old beater. He's oblivious to them. The way he's taking his time, you'd think he was the only one on the road. Why doesn't he put his truck in drive and step on the gas? The hound raises its head again and opens one eye, but then settles back onto the seat next to me. It reminds me of Rosie in a strange way. Rosie was a beagle with brown, white, and black patches. This dog doesn't have Rosie's colouring, but it's got her brown floppy ears and eyes that made you give in to her every time.

"Good boy," I say, giving the hound a light pat on the head. The dog offers a buffer, and I'm kind of glad for that. Same thing with Rosie when I'd take her to the park. People would stop and chat, and Rosie loved the attention. Most times I didn't say a word; didn't have to.

"Where ya headed?"

"Springfield." Slips off my tongue like it's a place I go all the time, no big deal.

The old guy nods, so I take it he knows where that is. "Well then, this must be your lucky day, because I'm going right past Springfield."

"Cool," I say, smiling.

The truck rumbles and vibrates, but the old guy doesn't seem to care. He rolls the window down a crack, and quickly lights up before putting the truck in drive. A thin stream of smoke gets sucked into the outdoors. I cough and look at the road ahead as he checks over his shoulder for oncoming traffic. Guilt stabs me in the chest as the truck pulls back onto the road. What's Mom doing right now? Is she wondering where I am, putting two and two together, figuring it all out—the reason I ran? And what about Dad? Is he okay? I can't believe I didn't put the stupid kit away. Just left everything in his room, then bolted.

"Heading to Waterloo, I can drop you off along the way."

I nod as if to say, who wouldn't know where Waterloo is? As for what he said earlier about this being my lucky day, if only he knew. This day is the beginning of the end for me; a beginning where no one knows where I've been and what I've done in my previous life.

I'm anonymous.

A clean slate—I like that.

"I'm Jack," I blurt out, suddenly compelled to say something because I just now got this super weird feeling that maybe I shouldn't be sitting in a stranger's truck, especially a stranger with a faded Shur-Gain logo on his cap and some unknown substance rolled up into a cigarette paper that's dangling from his lips. An axe murderer, an escaped convict, your run-of-the-mill pervert—from where I'm sitting, the possibilities seem endless. Mom would be having a fit if she knew. So would Dad, for that matter, even though he used to say that his summer hitchhiking was one of the best experiences of his life. But this isn't the eighties. And it's a whole other story when it's your kid out there doing his own thing.

"The name's Purchase," says the old guy. "James Purchase." He looks me up and down, then adds, "You're not from around these parts, are ya?"

I smile, cautious. I'm not sure what he's getting at, the real meaning behind him stopping to pick up some kid at the road-side who's not from *around these parts*; a kid who wasn't even thumbing a ride when he came along. Could be he has some secret plan to annihilate me. Kids disappear all the time. Lost. Forgotten. Wiped from the face of the earth. Bones discovered decades later when no one cares and the perp is long since dead. There won't be any point solving the crime.

My stomach churns. I don't want blowflies crawling up my nose, maggots feasting on my flesh and crawling into my body cavities. I think about the hidden weapon under his seat. The glove compartment. The waistband of his pants. There must be dozens of places to conceal an instrument of death.

The space in his smile makes him look like that charac-ter from *The Nightmare Before Christmas*. His eyes are sunken, expectant, like maybe I've got something he wants. A pause separates us. Another and another. And then he keeps on talking.

"Got a farm out in Waterloo. Lived there most all my life—adult life, that is. By myself, now that Edna's gone. Cancer. Ate her right up. Settled in her liver and kept on travelling."

Sun shines in through the windshield of the truck—blinding me. I squint. The dog lets out a long low groan and stirs for a moment before resuming its nap. James flips his visor down. More silence follows. Maybe he's waiting for me to say I'm sorry about his wife dying. Why else would he have shared all that? People enjoy talking about their own troubles. Not that they care about anyone else's. My friends stopped asking how things were at home. They even stopped dropping in to visit. Phone calls, texts trickled away. No one wanted to bother Sam now that his dad was sick.

James clears the phlegm from his throat and continues. "Not that Edna was a drinker, mind you, because she wasn't. Let's make that perfectly clear. Not a drop went past her lips. She wasn't a saint, I'm not saying she was, just didn't believe in putting that poison in her body. That's what she called it—poison. Three months and she was a goner. Makes you wonder how a person can be taken out so fast."

Three months is better than three years, I feel like saying. You can stretch a lot of grief out in three whole years. Grief should come when someone dies, not when they live. It's a messed-up way of thinking, I know that. But it's been my reality since Dad got sick, not that James needs to know any of this.

"On my way home from looking at a pair of steers in Maitland. I must be cracked in the head to even consider bringing something else home. Got too many creeturs to look after now."

I have no idea what creeturs or steers are. James is speaking a whole other language, but I keep quiet.

"Knees went out from under me awhile back and I've got no puff left in me...Emphysema, you understand, only they call everything nowadays that COPD. Time was you had asthma, bronchitis, or emphysema, or maybe all three if you were short on luck, but nope, they had to go change all that. Give it a bunch of fancy initials to cover it all."

There's a gurgling in his throat when he coughs. He tries to clear it a few times but can't get the phlegm loose. It's the grossest sound ever. At least James can actually cough, which is more than Dad can manage. Marcie pushes on his stomach, then uses suction. She even trained Mom how to do it. Luckily, *No suction* was on Dad's list for me.

"But...if it wasn't for farming, I don't know what else I'd do," James adds. "Just bury me in the manure pile when I croak." A wheezy laugh follows his words.

Don't ask me why, because I've only just met the guy, but I think he actually means it.

"Couldn't keep farmin' at all if it wasn't for Frankie helping out. Now, there's a body who doesn't mind getting their hands dirty. Hard worker, that one."

James's wrinkled hands twist on the steering wheel, making a squeaking sound. I shiver. They remind me of Grandpa Gillis's hands. Shaking that image from my head, I snap back to the present. Hopefully James won't run us off the road with his coughing and wheel twisting; bad knees and no puff. I glance over at him. His eyes are glued to the road ahead. Nothing he's said so far hints of an ulterior motive, so I relax a bit and try to quiet my mind the way I do during my sessions with Ms. Sandford.

Reach for a warm relaxing thought, Sam. Breathe slowly. Steadily. Release the pressure. Steady your mind.

A safe feeling settles over me. I glance back over at James. He's just a harmless old guy who likes to talk. No concealed weapons, just loneliness. Maybe this day won't be so bad after all.

CHAPTER 19

WE DRIVE ALONG FOR A FEW KILOMETRES, NOT SAY-
ing a whole lot of anything. We pass the sign that says
Springfield 10 km. and then James starts giving me a whole history lesson about the place. He talks about some big mill and
a place called Hastings. To hear him speak, it was some kind
of utopia. He tells me about the people who lived there, like
I'd know who they were. I zone out for a while, start thinking
about other things. I wonder if Dad misses all the long conversations he used to have with his clients, the witty comments he
could come up with at the snap of a finger; even the sound of
his own voice—his actual voice, that is. Having other people
around him besides Marcie, Mom, and me.

I look out the window while the old guy talks away. If it
makes him happy to spew out this stuff, so be it. Everyone
likes to show off the things they know, makes them feel
knowledgeable.

The countryside goes by in a blur. Fields, houses, and
barns—I'm not really focusing, just aware of what we're passing. I forgot how far out Lenny's camp is. Good thing James
stopped or I'd still be walking. We pass some Christmas trees
growing in a field. We always went to a U-pick and cut our
own tree, a Christmas tradition that got changed after Dad
was diagnosed. Mom ordered an artificial tree with lights from
Amazon without even discussing it with us. It arrived at the
house in a long, thin box and she asked me to help put it up.

"Looks great," said Dad.

Great? I wanted to twist the fake branches and break it through the middle. Our tree-cutting days were over. Family tradition went out the window. Yet we pretended that having an artificial tree was better than cleaning needles up off the floor.

As a family, we are good at faking.

James has gone quiet again, and for a time he looks like maybe he's a hundred miles away. I let him have his silence. Silence can be good at the right time. A bump in the road snaps him out of his trance and he starts yapping again.

"Mind me asking what you're doing out here by yourself?" I look over at him. I was hoping he wouldn't ask. There's this look on his face. He's suddenly suspicious, I'm just a trouble-making city kid up to no good. I've got to come up with something.

"No big deal," I tell him. "I come out to Lenny Porter's camp all the time. I had a few days off school. Professional development days." All the time? Professional development? Seriously? I glance over at James. Does he even know what a professional development day is? "It's nice down by the lake. Not that Lenny's camp is all that special."

"Is that a fact? So, you know Lenny?"

"Enough for him to let me stay in his camp a few days, so I guess so. It's all cool. I checked it out with him first. I used to come out here with my dad. He goes hunting with Cal and Jeff. Do you know them?" This isn't a complete lie. I'm sure Lenny wouldn't mind me staying in his camp a few days, at least until I come up with a long-term plan for the rest of my life. While he might not know me personally, he obviously knows Dad— or I should say, knew Dad, back in the old hunting days.

"Cal and Jeff? Nope, can't say I do." James nods while doing this funny thing with his bottom lip. It's making sense to him now. He's got no reason to doubt my story. That puts an end to his questions. From then on, we make small talk.

According to James, Lenny pulled off some wild stunts back in the day.

"A good guy, though," James adds. "Give you the shirt off his back."

"Good old Lenny," I say, smiling to make it look as though I know what he means.

When we hit Springfield, James offers to drop me off at the Sawmill Road. It's not on the main drag, but he says he doesn't mind. He stops the truck and it's time for me to get out. By this time he's kind of grown on me. The hound lifts its head, looks at me with its Rosie-like eyes, maybe begging me not to go.

"See you around, Jack," the old guy says. I grab my bag and pull up on the door handle. For a few seconds we look at each other like we've got unfinished business. Looking away, I thank him for the ride, give the hound a gentle pat on the head, and slam the door shut. I feel bad lying to James. But some lies are essential. I can't let anyone know my real name. The tailgate of his truck disappears from sight. I watch the dust rise from his tires.

This is it. Solitude. I hook my backpack over my shoulder. I'm all alone.

I turn and start down Sawmill Road, hoping my memory won't fail me, that I'll find Lenny's hunting camp no problem. A sign says *Sleepy Hollow* and there's a wide path lined with bushes on both sides. This might be the driveway, although I wouldn't exactly call it a driveway. It's barely wide enough for a car—maybe a four-wheeler. Nature changes over time. Trees grow and weeds push up through the gravel. But I remember now—or at least I think I do. I'm pretty sure this is the road, only it was definitely wider. Dad drove the Jeep right up the camp.

If there's any more luck in this day, I won't end up lost in the wilderness. Ten seconds in and I'm surrounded by trees. No camp in sight. Birds are singing from the branches, moving from limb to limb. I walk along, creeped out by this feeling that I'm being followed. What made me think I could last in the wild? I'm not used to roughing it. Dad showed me a few things, but if I get lost, I'll be cream peas on toast, as Marcie would say. Shaking off the creepy thoughts, I take out my iPod, stick the earbuds in, and hit play. Nothing. I remember then the battery is dead. Raising my head, I keep walking. I can do this.

CHAPTER 20

THE CAMP DOESN'T HAVE A LOCK, SO I TRIP THE latch. The same creepy feeling hits me when I open the door, like I'm not alone. Something suddenly scurries across the rafters. I suck in a breath, which is lot better than letting out a scream, even if there isn't anyone within earshot. Whatever it is runs down the wall. I take a jump back as it dashes toward me and out the door. I whirl around to see what it is. Two squirrels race up the trunk of a tree and disappear among the leaves.

"Dumb rodents," I grumble. Scaring the crap out of me like that. My heart finds a slower pace. They're sitting on a branch—show-offs—going ballistic, chattering. They're pissed that I've invaded their space.

"What's your problem?" I yell out at them. They've got no right taking over Lenny's camp like that. "You're trespassing, you know!"

I race down off the doorstep and find a stone, throw it in their direction but miss. Not that I want a squirrel's blood on my hands, but what were they doing in the camp in the first place? Animals live outdoors. Jillian March has a rabbit running loose in her house, but at least it's litter-trained and came from a pet store; it's had its shots.

I reach for another stone. Stop myself. I'm being ridiculous. Wasting my time trying to scare off a couple of squirrels, what's the point? There's a straw broom just outside the camp.

I start sweeping away the cobwebs stretched across the doorway. At least it was just squirrels. Could have been worse, as in raccoons or skunks, but that's as far as I'm going with that. This *is* the middle of nowhere. Hard to tell what all could be out here.

I step inside, checking that the coast is actually clear this time. Seeing no more rodents—no sounds or movements—I shut the door. The squirrels are acting like lunatics, chirping and chattering outside the camp. They're telling me to get lost. I'm the enemy. Well, too bad.

The year I came here with Dad, we shared the camp with Cal and Jeff. They were so different from Dad, who didn't drink or swear. I wonder how they had stayed friends all those years. I'm pretty sure Dad's hunting trips had nothing to do with hunting. He loved being in nature, getting away from the city. Jeff and Cal were hilarious, always making stupid jokes. Somehow Dad fit in there, but only to a degree. Friendships are complicated. I think about Noah; how much of our friendship was about hockey and nothing else? He's not interested in my writing.

"None of the comforts of home," Dad said when he swung the door open that first time. "No TV, computers, or video games. No electricity, cell service, or running water. You know what that means, don't you, Sam? No bathroom either. Think you can handle it?"

I didn't say anything. I could be tough even if that meant crouching in the bushes to take a crap. But then he burst out laughing and pointed toward a tiny square building that was dark and smelly inside. I laughed, a bit relieved. Even a hole in some boards is better than backing your butt up into the bushes.

A weekend without TV was a challenge. Dad brought along a set of walkie-talkies. Seemed kind of ancient, but with no cell service they did the job. It wasn't as if I was going to help track a deer or stumble around the woods after Dad. My job was to stay at the camp with Rosie along with strict instructions not to venture too far and to wear my hunter's orange vest and hat at all times. The hat and vest were essential regardless of how much of a geek I looked like wearing them.

"Think you're old enough for the responsibility, Sam?" Dad was talking to me man to man. I nodded because, man to man, I was more than ready. Mom wouldn't have agreed to Dad leaving Rosie and me at the camp alone. Maybe she thought Dad came out here to look at the trees and walk through the woods. No way were we going to tell her any details about our hunting trip when we got back home. Not sure she grasped what a hunting trip was all about anyway. Dad never came home with any carcasses. He'd just gather up his hunting gear and drive off for a few days.

The squirrels are outside, still going at it. Dropping my backpack onto the bed, I whirl around and stick my head out the door. "Chill out! No one's going to hurt you," I yell out at them. I stop. Who am I, Dr. Dolittle? I need to get a grip. I start checking things out in the camp instead. At least that makes sense.

The camp is musty and dank, the way places are that have been closed up tight—although obviously not tight enough to keep out rodents. I do a quick check for mice turds but don't see any, then go for the window to let in some fresh air. Man, this place is stale.

The window is hard to budge and squeaks as it begins to move. There's a piece of kindling lying on the window sill. I manage to raise the window and shove it underneath to hold the window in place. The breeze blows inward and I stand there for a bit. It feels good on my face; relaxing. The dingy green curtains flap up and down. The camp is smaller than I remember and not nearly as cool. It's actually kind of run-down and decrepit. Feels like I'm the only one aware of its existence. How long has it been since someone besides squirrels stayed here?

I sit on the bed, take out my notebook, and start writing: *Made it to the camp. Country people are far too trusting. James Purchase—good-hearted but gullible. Will come up with a strategy. Need to keep my head. Hope Mom and Dad are okay.*

I leave the notebook on the bed and take a closer look at my surroundings. Strange, how your perspective on things can change as you age. When I was ten, I was totally convinced that Lenny's camp was the coolest place in the entire universe. Now, not so much.

CHAPTER 21

MY STOMACH RUMBLES. SLINGING MY BACKPACK onto the table, I start rooting through my stash of food. I take out the bag with the trail mix and beef jerky but have a quick thought: there might be food in the cupboards. Conserving what I've got is probably wise. I have no idea how long I'll be here and what I'll do once the food runs out. There's a small country store not far from here, but the money I have left won't buy much. I'll have to choose wisely. Dad picked up odd jobs when he thumbed across Canada. Maybe that's an option, except I'm not sure how to go about doing that. Can't put a notice up at the store since they'd have no way to contact me. And do I really want anyone to know where I am? James does, but he doesn't seem like the sharpest tool in the shed.

I open the cupboard door above the sink. Nothing but cups and saucers with faded roses, some plates, and glasses that look as though they haven't been used in months—make that years. There's a small sealed jar filled with matches, some gauze tea bags in a plastic container, a tiny jar of instant coffee. I take the top off the coffee and give a sniff. Gross. I put it back on the shelf, then suddenly stop. I feel like an intruder. I've got no business helping myself to what's here. But then, who's going to care? By the looks of it, no one's been here in ages.

Below the sink I strike gold: beans in molasses, a can of peaches in light syrup, and sardines. The sardines will be a last resort and only if I'm about to croak from starvation. I shake the can of peaches. No point checking the date. Some things you don't need to know. Dates are only a suggestion anyway. Canned goods last forever.

The rusty can opener on the cupboard keeps slipping off the ridge of the can when I try turning it. Seems a lost cause. But then it finally punctures the lid and I open it enough to wedge a spoon into the hole. I eat straight from the can. Not bad, but then I haven't had any real food since before noon. M&Ms don't count. If I were home, I'd be chowing down on a pastrami sandwich, maybe even a slice of pizza in front of the TV. My stomach rumbles again. This kind of thinking doesn't help.

I wipe my chin in the crook of my arm and set the empty can on the table. What am I supposed to do now that I'm standing in the middle of this countrified structure with peach juice dribbling down my chin? Why did I come here in the first place? I guess when you want to escape, any place is better than the place you're at.

Maybe I watch too much sci-fi, but the first time I came here I felt like a time traveller. I pretended I was walking through the portal of one world and entering a whole other dimension. I don't know how else to describe it. Rosie felt it too, the way she looked up at me and whined that first time. Me and Dad laughed because it was kind of funny, Rosie saying, "You've got to be kidding me."

I'm actually kind of disappointed. I thought once I got to the camp it was going to be so great, that everything would be better. I have a lot of good memories of this place. Now I'm not so sure. Back at the house, all I thought about was getting away...and fast. I don't know of a lot of places to hide out.

I have a sudden need to kick something as I look around at my new reality. Two double beds with homemade quilts on them and a cot in the corner, an old kitchen table with five wooden chairs—two have the backs broken. There's a wooden bench with drops of blue paint on the seat. Rosie would crawl beneath it at night and drift off to sleep. In the middle of the room is an old woodstove and a supply of firewood in a metal tub beside it; a rusty stovepipe runs up through the ceiling. Not sure I've got it in me to start a fire, although you never know what you're capable of until you're forced into trying.

There's a kitchen sink with a small stain on the white enamel, but no running water. No water, period. The camp is below basic, but I have to take it. At least until I decide what to do next. Like speeding down the ice with the puck, I got here without really knowing how. Now that I'm completely alone, I'm not sure what to do.

The springs squeak as I stretch out on one of the beds. Arms behind my head and feet crossed, I stare up at the ceiling. Cobwebs hang from the rafters. Dead flies dangle in midair. No squirrels at least. I close my eyes, trying to empty my mind. No easier here than in Sandford's office.

"You're overthinking this, Sam Gillis. Just relax and let go," Ms. Sandford used to remind me each time. She has a habit of looking out over her glasses, which makes her seem older. You can tell the people who aren't here to impress; they go through life not caring what the world thinks. Kind of like Jody from the bus, and James, now that I think of it.

There's a strange buzzing sound above me. I try to locate its source. In the corner, near the ceiling—a housefly struggles to escape from a web. I watch it for a while, spinning in circles. I laugh, secretly glad for the distraction. But after a few minutes my mind clicks in. Really? Is this my entertainment now—a couple of psycho squirrels and a buzzing fly? I sit up, swinging my legs over the side of the bed. I might just die of boredom if I don't do something soon.

My tongue and throat are dry as dust. Shouldn't have eaten those M&Ms earlier. I root through my backpack for the water I picked up at the Big Stop. I twist the top, taking a small sip. It's warm but at least it's wet. But there isn't enough to get me through one day. At this point, water's more important than food. I read that humans can go twenty-one days without food but only three or four without water. Why didn't I think about that back at the Big Stop?

I step out onto the deck, trying to figure out how to get water. I know now what those people on *Survivor* go through. Hopefully I won't end up chowing down on strange bugs or rodents and drinking water from a ditch. I shake my head. Gotta stop these weird thoughts. Less than half an hour in the wilderness and I'm becoming unhinged. I go back to the problem—getting water. The lake's not far from here, but no way am I drinking blue-green algae. Worst-case scenario, I could boil it, that's if I can get a fire going in the stove. On second thought, drinking water from the lake would have to be an absolute last resort. As in, I'm about to die from thirst at this very moment.

The year I came here with Dad we signed a petition up at the convenience store to have the lake cleaned. There were hundreds of names on it. I'm pretty sure nothing came of it except maybe it got some of the locals excited for a time, thinking they were going to make a difference.

A light bulb suddenly goes off. There's a spring nearby; a small deep hole in the ground with clean water. Lenny got it checked out each year to make sure it was okay to drink. It probably hasn't been tested for years but, at this point, I'm willing to chance it. There was an old pail hanging on a bush that I used for dipping in the water. Maybe it's still there. Rosie and I would make water runs. Is it even possible for me to find the spring after all this time?

I scan the area, look to my right and left. It's got to be here somewhere. But I have no idea where. Stepping off the deck, I check around, looking for something familiar. The squirrels are still in a tree making noises. I tell them to shut up again and they go ballistic. Kinda like Rosie whenever she saw someone or something in the distance. You couldn't get her to stop barking.

Feeling a bit creeped out, I turn quickly to make sure no one's behind me. Nothing but trees and bushes, no movement in the distance. I've got to get a grip.

Locating the footpath that goes to the lake, I follow it through a thick wooded area until I reach the sandy beach. The lake is farther away from the camp than I remember. Running the distance with Rosie on a leash made it seem shorter.

I shake my head. I've got to stop imposing my fourteen-year-old self onto my ten-year-old memories. I'm not that same kid; four years and ALS have seen to that.

Down by the lakeshore, the wind has picked up, coming around the cove, pushing and shoving like an overgrown bully. It whistles around my ears. In the distance I hear traffic—proof there's life out there somewhere. A horn from a passing vehicle is barely audible. Still, it lets me know I'm not completely alone. There are people out there beyond the trees, even if I'm not a part of the action. It's probably safer that way. I need to keep a low profile.

I continue to study the shoreline. The fall we came here, Rosie chased the waves, finding sticks along the beach for me to throw. She'd run out into the lake, her short legs pulling her through the water while I cheered her on. We played there for hours. Tongue out, legs sprinting, zigzagging along the shore—she'd suddenly turn and run back into my arms, knocking me down as she licked my face.

Picking up a stick, I throw it as far as I can, listening to Rosie barking as she races along the water's edge—a ghost of a memory that leaves a hard knot in my throat. I kick at a clump of grass. I'm being stupid.

I sit in the sand staring out at the water. The lakeshore is deserted, nothing but a few birds in the sky, fighting against the wind. Late October, and the cottages are closed up, everything packed away for another season.

There's a peacefulness in nature you don't get anywhere else. Four years ago I wasn't paying attention. I get why Dad liked coming here. Rosie and me were too busy running and playing to appreciate it. Ten-year-olds don't take time to reflect.

The water is choppy and I watch the coloured leaves across the lake, quivering. But this is getting me nowhere. I jump to my feet and knock the sand off my butt. Enough of this reminiscing, already. It's time to get busy. Find some water before I die of thirst.

I walk through the bushes, looking for the path that leads to the spring. It's got to be here somewhere. Paths last forever. It's not like someone could have moved it. Something catches my eye in the bushes ahead. I keep going, gulp in air. Sunlight reflects off a metal bucket hanging from a tree branch. The spring! I hurry toward it. The sound of running water comes from deep in the ground. I set aside the crude wooden cover and scoop out the dead leaves the way Dad showed me when I was ten. I take the bucket and dip into the cool dark water. This day might be crazy, but I won't die of thirst.

CHAPTER 22

COMING TO THE CAMP MIGHT NOT HAVE BEEN SUCH a good idea. Too much to think about—Rosie, Dad, hockey—they're all haunting me. Thinking about it over and over won't change anything. Wish it could. Einstein said insanity is doing the same thing over and over and expecting a different outcome. Maybe the same thing could be said about thinking the same thing over and over.

Setting the notebook aside, I take the small framed photo of Rosie and me out of my backpack. It was taken on the front steps of the camp. The last picture of us together. I suddenly wish I could go back in time. I'd change some things about that day if I could. I set the photo on the table. Take out the box with Rosie's name on it. Brush my fingers across the smooth wood grain and set it beside the photo.

All this thinking has made me famished again. I go back to the cupboard and check out the few options I have. Beans in molasses sauce, but I'm not eating them cold. I consider making a fire in the stove.

The year I came here with Dad, he used kindling and bits of bark to start a fire. It was the coolest thing. That's when I really got it. Dad could actually survive in the wilderness. He was a natural. Like Davy Crockett, minus the coonskin cap, like in that old black-and-white movie we watched one Friday night. Why was I just finding that out? Wish now I had taken Dad up on his offer to show me how to start a fire. Who knew it'd be a skill I'd need one day?

I make up my mind to stop being a kid. I need to survive. Dad's not here to help out. It's just me. There are sticks on the ground outside the camp. Gathering a supply, I open the stove lid and push some into the hole. I need something to light the fire.

Matches. There are some in a jar up in the cupboard. I go for them, but stop. I almost forgot. Dad used birchbark. There was a white birch along the trail leading to the camp.

"Sorry," I whisper as the bark comes free. I stop. What's got into me? Talking to squirrels, apologizing to a tree. I shake my head. I really am a city kid.

It's not long before a fire is burning in the stove. It wasn't as hard as I thought. Maybe I *am* cut out for this. Getting back to my original mission of heating the beans, I grab the worn can opener. A hundred tries later, I manage to open the can far enough to get the beans out. I dump them into a pot I find sitting on a shelf. While waiting for them to warm, I rip into the Oreos. I stop myself from eating them all. Best to save some for later. I fold the top down to keep them fresh, then grab a plate and teacup from the cupboard. There's a metal scoop on the counter. I dip into the bucket of spring water, pour some into the teacup. Grabbing my notebook and pen, I take my food and sit out on the deck. I quickly realize that it's quiet out here. I actually wouldn't mind a little noise. I check out the tree branches for movement, but the squirrels are nowhere to be seen. I stuff the beans in my mouth and gulp down the water. Eating doesn't take long without Mom and Dad asking about my day. Setting my empty plate down, I pick up my notebook.

—

Rosie would pull on the leash like she was the boss. She probably was. In every dog/owner relationship, someone needs to be. For a small dog, she knew how to get her own way. She decided when to stop, when to go, who to bark at, what to sniff, when and where to poop. I just followed along. I was eight. What did I know about leading back then? Some days I'd try to take charge, show her I was the boss, something every good dog owner should do. I wanted to be a good dog owner. I wanted Rosie to listen when I spoke.

She'd resist every time, bracing her feet, lunging at Sparkie, who was two sizes bigger, when we walked down the sidewalk. She'd bark like she was never going to stop. I'd tell her to quiet down. But Rosie never paid much attention to my commands. She knew what she wanted and for the most part it was simple: to play and run and come back to a bowl of food that was waiting for her in the corner of the kitchen. And most of all, she wanted to be free.

I stop writing. Looking back, I can't blame Rosie for any of that. I haven't felt this light for a long time. I set the notebook aside and sit back with my feet on the railing.

Freedom—I could get used to this.

CHAPTER 23

MY STOMACH'S FULL, AND CONTENTMENT HAS replaced the earlier rumbles. I flip through my notebook and look at what I've written. The pages are filling up. I'd only planned to write brief notes, but without my laptop for the serious writing, I've got no choice. I'll keep the writing small. Hopefully, I can make it out later. I'll admit, it felt good writing about Rosie.

I've put it off for too long. That sounds stupid, I know, but purging on paper is brutal. I wasn't ready until now.

There was no time to think about Rosie once ALS showed up. Rosie got filed away under "unfinished business" while I spent my time trying to understand my dad's disease. One day I'll write about that, the way Ms. Sandford said, but right now, I'll stick to Rosie's story. Too much truth could cause a system overload.

I head down off the deck to go exploring, taking my notebook along just in case. I bet Hemingway never let his notebook out of his sight. Inspiration hits at the oddest times; a writer needs to be prepared. Guess that's me: ex–hockey star turned writer. And some of my best stuff comes when I'm not thinking about anything in particular.

I noticed another path when I was going to the outhouse earlier. It might be interesting to see where it leads. James said there was a mill around here about a hundred years ago. The way he talked, it was a big deal. Hard to believe with all the trees and bushes growing here now.

The woods are quiet. I wonder where those lunatic squirrels are? They could be plotting their next attack or be off pestering someone else—if there's even anyone out here within a ten-kilometre radius. I check out the branches above me as I hike along. Still no squirrels, but that doesn't mean something else isn't out there waiting to pounce. I've seen movies where cougars jump out of the trees in front of travellers, although the experts can't agree as to whether we have any here in Nova Scotia. Depends upon who you ask. Jeff claimed he saw one years ago. "Whatever it was, it was big. Like nothing I've seen before," he said. Dad sounded skeptical. "You're sure it wasn't a sasquatch?" he said. Cal and I laughed like fools.

I walk through the trees, paying close attention to my surroundings. I don't want to get lost. Dad used to say that nature provides her own road signs, and to look for markers when you're out in the woods, especially if you're alone. I sure wouldn't mind stumbling across some weird-looking rock or tree right about now. I finally see a big birch, twisted and gnarled. It has a black growth on the side—chaga, it's called. One of the natural remedies Mom made Dad try when he was first diagnosed. A cure for everything, but apparently not ALS. Not sure how much chaga tea Dad drank, but it was a lot.

That wasn't the end to the natural remedies. Over the next year, Mom made him try a bunch of weird herbs, but she finally gave up. None of it was helping. Dad wasn't into that natural stuff anyway, but he didn't want to disappoint Mom. "It makes her feel helpful," he said.

From out of nowhere, I hear some weird sounds in the distance. I stop to listen. Birds start singing, louder as they move through the trees behind me. Then all at once they go ballistic, wings beating, chirping like crazy. They're heading my way. Maybe they're being chased by something, but what? It's like some weird wilderness overload, something straight out of Hitchcock. Maybe they've joined forces and are on the attack, searching out animals and humans in their path. Leaves rustle. Some fall to the ground. There's a loud fluttering of wings overhead. They're directly above me now. There's got to be hundreds...make that thousands. I cover my head with my arms—a gut reaction—as I prepare to be attacked. My eyes squeeze tight. No way do I want them pecked out. I need my eyes if I'm going to make it out of here.

The squawking gets louder as more birds soar through the trees. I'm on the brink of annihilation, like in the movie we watched a few weeks back. Only I'm being attacked by a bunch of killer birds, not a pack of wild dogs. I fall to my knees waiting for the end to come...

Still waiting...

But then everything gets quiet. I look up into the trees. A few more leaves flutter to the ground, an afterthought. The birds have passed through. I jump up and brush some dead leaves off my jeans. There comes more tweeting. A lone straggler bringing up the rear. I can't help it. I burst out laughing. This is usually where you find out you've been punked. Your most embarrassing moment ends up all over social media. I look around. I don't see anyone. Not one of my more stellar moments. At least it was private, between me, the trees, and the killer birds. Not like the night Noah thought he heard the bear in our backyard.

Instead of going back to the stuffy old camp, I decide to keep going. If I get turned around, I'll be sunk. An outdoorsman I'm not. But come on, surely I can keep myself alive out here. At least until I figure out what I'm going to do with the rest of my life.

The rest of my life? I gulp. Weird. I wasn't thinking about that when I took off this morning. What *will* I do with the rest of my life?

Mom's going to send the cops after me for sure. Then what? Will I get found out and end up thrown in jail? Well, maybe not jail, but juvie. Am I a delinquent?

I stop. I've got to get real, use my head. No one's going to come looking for me here. It's been ages since Lenny's camp was mentioned in our house. They'll check with my friends first, places in the city, and by then I'll be out of here.

But that's not even the worst possibility. What if I get lost in the woods? I could end up a bunch of bones discovered years down the road. All I wanted was to get away, clear my brain, have no responsibilities...not end up a dead body deep in the woods.

I try to push these weird thoughts out of my head, but it's not easy.

Finally, I stumble upon a nice gravel road and start down it. I pick up speed. It's all okay. I've been on this road before. Up ahead is the rock I sat on while Rosie explored the shoreline. I hurry toward it. It kind of looks like a chair with a scooped-out place to sit and even a back. Hard to miss. I called it our rock, even though we were only there two days and Rosie hardly spent any time sitting on it. She just walked along with her nose down, sniffing everything she could find. When we heard a shot far off in the distance, she froze. A few times she took off running and barking, but as soon as I called for her she came back. It was kind of amazing. If she'd been back home she'd never have stopped. It was as if she belonged in the wilderness more than she did the city.

I take out my notebook and jot down a few sentences, memories from our days at camp—Rosie and me—then sit back on our rock and relax. I think over my present situation again. I can't stay at the camp for long. Gotta have food, and my supply isn't plentiful. Plus, I can't live the rest of my life out here.

The wind has calmed and the lake is almost still now. Pretty oranges and reds stretch out through the trees as the sun sinks farther down. Dad and I sat by the lake before dark and watched the sunset.

Somewhere behind me, the chattering starts up. The squirrels must have followed me to the lake, probably making fun of me, stuck out here in the middle of nowhere. Ignoring them, I jot down some notes about my newfound survivor skills. Maybe one day it'll be important.

I can take the squirrels' noise for only so long. I close my notebook. There've got to be better nature sounds out here. Grabbing a small rock, I throw it at them. I'm way off, never could throw for beans. That's why I went for hockey, that and the fact that I wanted to be the next Sidney Crosby. The squirrels race off, jumping from limb to limb. I look around. It's getting late. I hurry toward the camp. When I reach the clearing, I look around for any signs of life. It's deserted. Not sure what I expected. The squirrels might be annoying, but at least they're company. I turn back toward the door, but stop. Did something just race behind the camp? I call out Rosie's name. That weird feeling hits me in the gut again. I shake it off, run up the steps, and quickly close the door. Coming here is feeling like a big mistake.

I throw myself onto the bed. That hunting weekend with Dad, I had no idea it would be our first and last trip to the camp, Rosie and me. Why did I think coming here now would be a good idea?

CHAPTER 24

EVENING CREEPS IN, TAKING UP SPACE INSIDE THE camp. I get up and look out the window. There's nothing left of the sunset; not much light coming in through the windows now. Darkness gathers in the corners. I consider opening the door to let in more light. The solitude and darkness are weirding me out. But then, an open door might seem like an invitation to wild animals. Squirrels are bad enough. I'm sure there are plenty of other beasts out there just waiting for a place to curl up for the night.

My stomach rumbles, reminding me it's time to eat again—like I've ever in this lifetime needed reminding. There are still cookies in the bag, but I've got to watch my food supply. I grab the beef jerky and head out onto the deck. Maybe tomorrow I'll walk out to the convenience store.

The jerky is chewy. Just what I need to keep myself occupied while considering my options. Not quite sure what to do with the rest of my life. I can't go back in time, even if I wanted to. The only place for me is forward. The breeze feels refreshing. I lean against the deck post and bite off another piece of jerky. I'm not ready to call it a night, so I stay outside listening for those stupid squirrels. They're nowhere to be seen. And if they were close by, I'd know it by sound anyway. Nothing but a bird squawking in the background. Figures. Where are the dumbass rodents when you want them?

I wait for the first star in the night sky. Dad started showing me the constellations when I was four. We didn't have a real good view of the night sky, not like out here in the wild, but we made do. We'd look through the telescope on Saturday nights, so late that Mom would come out onto the deck and make us come in. Rosie would be outside with us, usually curled up near my feet. "It's time Sam was in bed," Mom would say, and I'd beg her to give us ten more minutes.

I stare out at the night sky. Feels like it could swallow me up and no one would ever know what became of me. I sit on the steps. In the distance, an owl hoots. Nature sure has some unusual sounds. There's the occasional noise of traffic in the distance. It's the night air, the direction of the breeze making it seem farther away than it is. A part of me wishes I could stay here forever. The other part, the logical part, knows full well that's impossible.

Stars continue to fill up the sky one by one. The moon's round face stares down at me. Rustling in the bushes to my right stops me mid-chomp. I wait to hear more but realize what a stupid move that is. I grab the empty food wrapper, squeeze it into a ball, and jump to my feet. Hurrying inside the camp, I throw the garbage in the stove. I go through the drawers looking for something, I'm not sure what. I can barely see what I'm doing, but I need to do something. This solitude stuff is overrated.

A kerosene lamp is on the table. I remove the glass shade. Dad let me do this, so I actually know what I'm doing. I light the wick and put the shade back in place, set the lamp in the middle of the table. I look around. The light casts a soft glow on the walls. Better, but not perfect. Opening my notebook, I jot a few things down. An electric lamp has a lot over a kerosene one. In the dim light it's hard to see. I wonder how the old-timers lived years ago. Probably James was one of them. They didn't purposely choose to live off the grid. There was no grid. But I guess you can't miss what you've never had. I've heard it called "simpler times," but it sounds more like "boring times."

If I don't die from starvation first, boredom will take me out for sure. Things here are totally different without Jeff and Cal and Dad sitting around telling their stories. I shouldn't have come, but where else would I have gone? When you're a fugitive, you can't stay in one place for long. I've seen enough movies to know that.

Finding a beat-up deck of cards in one of the drawers, I remove the elastic holding them together and sit down at the table. I try laying them out for solitaire, but it's hard to see with just a kerosene lamp. I look down at the cards. This is stupid. I can't remember what to do next. Dad told me where to place the cards—red on black, black on red. But without him here, I've got nothing.

I turn the lamp wick down to conserve the kerosene and crawl into bed. The lamp gives very little light—still better than complete darkness, except now I can't shut my freaking mind off. Tossing and turning, I finally give up on sleep. I lie in the dark, thinking about this morning, going over it all in my head.

I know Dad's health has been failing and that he hasn't been working as much as he was, but I wasn't expecting him to order one of those kits I heard him talk about with Mom. What's going to happen to him now? Mom won't be able to help him. She told him that three years ago, and she was crying to Marcie the other day, saying, "I can't. I just can't." The kit was out on the counter, what else would she have been upset about?

This whole thing with Dad, him wanting to die with dignity, the kit showing up...I didn't think things through. Seeing Grandpa Gillis take his last breath haunted me for a long time. I can't go through that again. I thought I was ready, all the talks we had about medically assisted death. What a laugh. I've failed Dad *and* Mom. Not only that, they'd say I should have come to them so we could sort it out together. Even if I wanted to, I can't go back. I can't be there when Dad dies. I know that now.

With me out of the picture, what will Dad do? He for sure won't ask Marcie to help him die. There's no one else. Rupert? He's too old to go to jail. After all my big ideas on dying with dignity, my participation in the rally, I'm not ready to say goodbye. Not one bit.

I turn over in bed and then it hits me. If I never go back, it'll be like Dad's still alive, doing his legal aid work and fighting for all the causes he believes in. I'll just think about the good times, before ALS, the places we went, the hockey games, the stupid things we laughed about, be the family we were. I remember Dad saying after Grandpa Gillis died that people live forever in our memories, and that's right. If I never go home, Dad can live forever.

Tomorrow morning I'll figure out my next move. I settle down into the mattress, pull the quilt around me. I can't stay out here in the sticks forever. And while I'm not one hundred percent positive, I think it's safe to say that this day will go down in history as one of the worst of my life. But right now, in this moment, I'm okay.

CHAPTER 25

I WALK THROUGH THE PRISON DOORS LIKE I'VE DONE it a hundred times before. The guards seem to know me; they nod as I pass by, one of them smiles. They look tough, but I don't let myself be intimidated. I walk up to the prison cell and grab hold of the bars. There's this guy sitting on a cot, in a prison uniform, his head hanging down. He looks up at me and I can't look away. His eyes are lifeless, not a spark left in there. He's hollow inside and there's no hope left in him.

"Do you have any regrets?" I say and he shakes his head.

"I didn't do anything wrong," he replies, and I can tell he believes what he's saying.

"That's not what the law says." My words come out cold and harsh.

He stands up from the cot and walks toward me. He looks directly into my eyes.

I sit up in bed. My heart's doing weird things. I'm not sure where I am, but then it comes to me. There's barely enough light to see by, and I want light. The lamp looks like it's dying, and then I remember that I adjusted the wick before bedtime to save kerosene. Jumping out of bed, I rush over to the table and turn the wick back up. I think about the dream, about the sad look in the dude's eyes when he looked at me. I know who he is. I'm the dude behind the bars, but I'm a lot older than I am now.

—

Morning comes and sunlight shines through the window. Pre-dawn, Dad used to call it, those mornings he drove me to the rink. I called it "getting up too early," but it meant getting in some ice time. I'll admit, we saw some pretty awesome sunrises back then. Now, the only thing waking me up too early are my thoughts. I wasn't sure I'd be able to fall asleep last night, and then that stupid dream woke me up. Just what I needed. But now I gotta push all those thoughts aside and *concentrate on the present*, as Dad would say.

Plans...I need to plan where I'll go and what I'll do. I can't stay here for long. Someone's bound to come looking and I'll need more food soon. Eventually Mom will think about the camp. Someone could be on their way here now. But I can't face Dad. I let him down.

I try to come up with something solid, but my options are limited. In fact, they're almost nonexistent. Dad thumbed his way across Canada, taking the occasional bus when he had the money, but I'm out here in the wilderness where no bus would dare go. I'm actually homeless, like those people living in tents in the city.

Tents. That's it! Maybe I can earn some money and buy a tent to live in. But I don't know a soul here, let alone anyone who would have odd jobs for me to do. They'd question why I'm not in school. No way I can pass for eighteen. I wonder about leaving my name at the store, but is that wise? There's not even a number for anyone to call. How would they get in touch with me? Who would hire someone who doesn't have a phone? Dumbass idea, coming here in the first place. I pull the quilt around me and roll over in bed. I never thought being all alone would be so—I don't know—lonely and weird. Kind of like being in solitary confinement. No wonder I'm having strange dreams.

The lamp is still burning. There's not much oil left in it. It gets pretty dark inside the camp at night. Mom keeps a night-light out in the hallway at home.

I get up and blow out the lamp. If I stay here another night, I'll be sleeping in darkness. I'll have no choice. Another night—I don't like the sound of that. Maybe some moonlight will shine in the window. I hobble out onto the deck in my sock feet and take a leak. I glance around for the squirrels. Even they've deserted me. Good riddance. I crawl back into bed. The urge for more sleep overshadows my hunger. I stare up at the ceiling. It's warm beneath the quilts. Too bad I can't stay under here forever.

I must have dozed off, because the next thing I know I'm hearing noises from outside. I lie there stunned, trying to fig-ure out what's going on. Squirrels? No way. I sit up. A bear? That last thought sends my heart pounding. Now fully awake, I hear someone shouting. Something's rumbling in the dis-tance; a vehicle, maybe? It's followed by "Hey...I said, hey." The voice has a familiar ring, but that's impossible. I don't know anyone here. My heart goes ballistic as heavy boots clomp up the steps. That's it. I'm dead meat. Country people don't like trespassers. Dude's probably wielding a shotgun.

Someone knocks, rattling the door.

I jump out of bed, shove my feet into my sneakers, and start cramming things into my backpack like crazy. If I'm about to be murdered, I'm not going lie here and do nothing. I slip my backpack on, ready to make a break for it the moment the door swings open. Whoever is on the other side, they'll have to run me down.

"Are ya in there, Jack?"

Jack? I freeze in my tracks. What the...? James? It can't be. What's he doing here?

"Hang on a sec." I drop my things on the table and straighten the crumpled quilts on the bed. Not sure why I care if he sees that the bed's unmade. I've got no idea whether it's morning or afternoon. I swing the door open. I croak out his name but rein in my relief at seeing a friendly face. After the night I put in, I'm just happy to see anyone.

"You lost or something?" I try to make light of his sudden appearance. Truthfully, I'm relieved on so many levels. I wasn't expecting to ever see the old guy again.

"I can leave if you want," he shoots back. I smile at him. Maybe I should have started out with "Good morning."

"Listen, I got thinking after I dropped you off yesterday." He rocks back on his heels, takes his Shur-Gain hat off (partially bald head with a few wispy tufts of grey hair—figures), and scratches his head before replacing it. "If you're not too drove up right now, I could use your help on the farm for a few days. Can't pay a whole lot, but there's a cot in the kitchen."

"My help?" Is this for real?

"Yeah, help...You know, gathering eggs, shovelling shit— that sort of thing. Got a little firewood needs to be split and piled." I shift uncomfortably. Does he really need help or do I look like a charity case?

"What about that Frankie guy you mentioned yesterday? I thought he helps you out. As in, no one can work like Frankie." I stop. Maybe I shouldn't be reminding him. There's something Dad used to say about not looking into a horse's mouth, meaning you shouldn't question your good luck. I don't know anything about working on a farm. But then, James doesn't know I'm a city kid either, unless he's got a crystal ball. It didn't come up in our conversation yesterday.

"For your information, Frankie's busy for the next little while." James has this amused look on his face. So, that's it? I'm the consolation prize? Should have known.

He keeps talking. "Looks like you could maybe use a couple of warm meals thrown in, too. I'll tell you right now, I'm no master chef, you're not going to get any fixings like they make on those cooking shows, but I can throw things together in a pot and it's not all bad." He gives a small laugh.

I want to yell out "Hell yeah!" but don't. Too much enthusiasm will make me seem desperate, and who wants to look desperate—even in front of James? James waits for my answer, staring me down. Where's that amused look from a few moments ago? I've paused too long. He shrugs and says, "Fine by me, if you're not interested..." He puts his cap back on and I can't read his face. He turns back toward the truck.

So that's it? He's changed his mind and I'm out in the cold? Do I call out? Run after him?

Dumbass squirrels come out of hiding and start racing through the tree branches, chattering like imbeciles. Nice timing, a-holes. I've got to stop James. Charity or not, whatever he's offering sounds better than spending another night out in the boonies by myself, chowing down on outdated canned goods.

James continues on his way. I've got to do something—fast. It's not like someone else is going to come along with a better offer.

I let out a casual "Hey there." I've got to make like this is no big deal. I'm a fugitive. Being on the run means I've got to blend in, fly under the radar, not raise suspicions. James doesn't flinch when I call out. Crap. Either he didn't hear me or else he really *has* changed his mind.

"Wait up!" I call out, loud enough to be heard.

The old guy keeps walking. He's whistling a tune. He couldn't be happier. No way is he driving away without me.

When he opens the door and starts to climb in, I can see he's grinning.

"Whatcha waiting for?" he says, looking back at me.

"My things. They're inside."

He sticks his head out the truck window. "Make it quick. Ain't got all day. Time's a-wasting." He gives the horn a quick honk. I'm holding in laughter as I race back inside the camp. Making out he was going to drive away without me was obviously part of his plan to get me to come with him. Sneaky.

As I grab my backpack, I see the bag with my garbage on the counter and take it with me. I do a quick scan of the camp to make sure I'm not forgetting anything. All good. Everything's in its place. James honks the horn again just as I open the passenger's side of the truck. I climb in, smiling. *Smartass*, I want to say, but don't. He's old but he deserves my respect, and I'm too grateful.

"Say hello to Jack, Butch. He's going to be staying with us for a few days." The hound raises it head and looks at me. I can't help laughing when Butch stretches out his neck and lets out a quiet howl.

"Pleased to meet you, Butch," I say, giving one of his paws a shake. Nice to have an actual introduction. He groans and pulls back, puts his head back down on the seat, unimpressed.

"Whatcha got in that bag of yours?" says James.

"Can't leave garbage behind," I tell him.

He laughs. "Just throw it on back. I'll get it later."

I give it a toss and climb into the truck.

"All set?" he asks, looking over at me.

I fasten the seat belt. "Sure thing."

"Let's get on out to the old shack, then." He puts the truck in reverse, wearing a wide, mostly toothless grin. Old shack? I'm trying my best not to break into a smile, but I can't help it. Is this guy for real?

CHAPTER 26

JAMES TURNS THE TRUCK AROUND AND HEADS BACK out the narrow drive. Bushes scrape the sides of the truck. Good thing it's just an old beater. I look in the side-view mirror. The camp disappears from sight. Seeing it off in the distance reminds me of Dad all over again—all the things we've missed out on, and all the things I'll miss out on for the rest of my life. "Such a waste of time and talent," I once overheard Marcie say to Mom. But it's more than that, something I can't fully describe. Why is life so cruel? Dad never hurt anyone. In fact, he did a ton to help people. Thinking about it again makes me want to punch something, like maybe the dash. I shake it off, start thinking about Dad in the backyard sparking up the barbeque, healthy and strong, having the guys over like we used to. I turn and start watching the road ahead. I'm kind of glad to be getting away from here.

Coming to this cheesy old camp was a bad idea, but I had to go somewhere. The only thing cool about the camp was being there with Dad and Rosie, and hanging out with Cal and Jeff in the evening, listening to their stories. But then again, if I hadn't come here, I wouldn't have met James. I could still be walking the road, maybe even sleeping outside.

As the truck putters along, James dives into another one of his stories. I could pop in my earbuds to cut down the sound, but don't bother. No sense trying to shut him out. Besides, the battery in my iPod is toast. Maybe James will let me recharge once we get to his place. Truthfully, I don't mind his stories. And it would be rude, shutting him out with my music, him offering me a job and some meals. He probably won't pay much, but I can save up for the tent. Not only that, he might know someone else who needs a hand. It feels good to have a plan, even if it will take a while to make happen.

I wonder about his cooking skills. James doesn't look like someone who'd go to a lot of trouble. At this point, I don't care. Beats hanging out at some crappy old camp. And James probably doesn't get much chance to talk, at least to someone who can answer him back. He did his share of talking yesterday. He probably finds it lonely with his wife being dead.

He starts telling me about the years he spent farming, and how he couldn't see himself never keeping animals. It's kind of sad. All he's got are a bunch of cows and chickens to talk to, and Butch, of course. But honestly, Butch seems so out of it, I'm not sure how much company he is. Not only does he smell bad, but he's got to be like two hundred in dog years.

I start wondering what James's place looks like, him calling it "the old shack" the way he did. That and the fact that his wife's been dead for years now. Old guys like James probably don't do housework. I could be walking into a disaster area. Not that I'm a neat freak, but you just don't know. I've seen TV shows where people hoard weird things in their homes, stacks of empty toilet paper rolls or tin cans and plastic shopping bags, leaving only a narrow path to walk through. Some of them have to step over garbage to get from one messy room to the next. Who's to say James isn't one of them? I look over at him and decide he probably has more plastic shopping bags than Sobeys. This should be good.

James slows down the truck and puts the blinker on. The mailbox out by the road says *Purchase*. The letters are black and a bit crooked, like it was done by a little kid. As he turns down the driveway, my stomach makes a quiet rumble. James looks over at me and says, "You look like you could stand a little nourishment, Jack. Had anything to eat yet this morning?" I grin. I'm pretty sure he didn't hear my stomach growl. Unless he's got supersonic hearing, and not just good timing.

"I didn't have time," I say, hoping this means what I think it means. I'm starving.

"Hungry?"

Eager for a taste of something good, I nod, grinning like a gorilla. "I could eat a bear." A bear? Sheesh. Listen to me. Wow. I've hardly been away from the city twenty-four hours and already I'm talking country. Enough already.

There's a big white house off in the distance and I glance over at James. I hope bear's not actually on the menu.

"Home sweet home," he cackles, an unlit cigarette now dangling from his lip. Seems early in the morning to be smoking. The driveway is long and bumpy with lots of trees lining the way. Coloured leaves rustle. It's kind of nice, like *Anne of Green Gables*. Mom would love it. There's a big field not far in the distance. I lean in toward the windshield for a closer look at the animals. They're humongous. They must be those "creeturs" James was talking about yesterday? They look like regular cows to me. James is hard to understand. I could seriously use a translator. I got used to untangling some of Dad's sentences when his speech became slurred. Surely, I'll be able to catch on to James soon. At least enough so that I can figure out what he's saying. No one likes to keep repeating themselves. How many times can I say "What?" without getting on his nerves?

The mostly grey barn to my left hasn't seen a splash of paint in decades. I thought all barns were bright red. They were red in all the books Mom used to read to me when I was little.

The big surprise ends up being that "the old shack" isn't as shack-like as James made it out to be. It's not a palace, but I like the front porch and the huge windows. It's actually kind of cool. Reminds me a bit of the old houses we saw in Lunenburg the day the tall ships were in. The town is hundreds of years old. We spent as much time looking at the houses that day as we did the ships.

Butch leads the way. His tail has a serious rhythm going. Probably the fastest part on him. I bend down to scratch his head and tell him he's good boy. He licks my hand and looks up at the door. James turns the knob and Butch slips inside. James looks back at me.

"You coming?" I stand on the steps hanging fast to my backpack. Who doesn't lock their front door when they leave?

At this point, nothing about James would surprise me. He probably has the place booby-trapped, which is the real reason he doesn't lock his door. I cautiously walk inside. A woodstove is giving off a nice heat. The kitchen has a homey feel to it. There's an outdated chrome table and four chairs, red checkered curtains over the windows. I'm surprised there's not a hot apple pie cooling on a windowsill.

"Make yourself at home," says James, hobbling his way to the counter. I see then what he meant about having bad knees. I set my backpack on the cot by the woodstove. Butch finds his place in an old wicker basket near the foot of the cot while James dishes up breakfast—hardboiled eggs and some bacon that's been sitting out on the counter all this time getting cold. James puts two slices of bread in the toaster and nukes the bacon. He puts it on a plate along with the hardboiled eggs and waits for the toast to pop up. It's not long before the smoke is rolling. Sputtering, he scrapes the burnt toast over the sink before setting the plate down in front of me. The toast is darker than I like, but I'm not going to complain. Sure beats what's left in my backpack for food. I butter the toast and dive in. I stop suddenly and look up at James. He's not eating.

"Aren't you hungry?" I must look like a starving fool. Where are my manners? Mom would have a fit if she could see me right now.

"Et already," he says, pushing his lips together.

"Et?" What's he talking about? He walks over to the sink with the frying pan and reaches for a pot scrubber.

"Yeah...et. You hard of hearing or something? Now hurry and finish up. There's work to be done. This ain't no free ride. Let's get that part straight right off the bat."

I'm frozen. Where's the friendly old guy from yesterday?

He turns back toward me and waves me on. "I didn't bring you out here to taste-test the cuisine. We've got work to do."

I shovel in the rest of my breakfast, grab the milk, and chug it down. "Ready," I say, wiping my mouth on my jacket sleeve.

James pulls the glass from my fingers and whips my plate away. Two seconds later, he's putting them in the dishrack to dry. I follow him out into the yard. He opens the door to an old rundown shed and makes for me to look inside. It's jam-packed with garbage—all things no sensible person would ever save. There's a pile of old bags that have *Shur-Gain* written on them and a whole slew of things that are unidentifiable. At home, we have a few gardening tools and a lawn mower in our shed, but this, this is a disaster.

"Just stack everything outside for now," he says. "Put it in piles. Don't want to throw out anything good."

Good? It all looks like junk.

I work like a madman, flinging things outside. Midmorning, James goes into the house and brings out pepperoni and cheese. It's not cut up in slices or arranged in any particular manner the way Mom would do it, but it still tastes good.

"I've been meaning to clean the shed out for the longest while," he says, handing me a diet cola. I feel like reminding him that I'm doing all the work. He looks into the shed. There's a big smile on his face. I flip the top and take a sip.

It takes the rest of the morning, but when lunchtime rolls around the shed is cleaned down to the bare floor. Everything is stacked in neat piles outside, the way James wanted. Feels like an accomplishment. At least the work is keeping my mind off home. We head into the kitchen.

"Make yourself a sandwich." James opens the fridge and slaps a half-eaten roll of bologna in my hands. "Newfie steak," he cackles.

Remembering his early bossiness, I give a light laugh to humour him. Next comes the mustard and mayo. I can't remember the last time I ate bologna. There was a whole list of foods Mom stopped buying after Dad got sick. Truthfully, I don't miss it. No one actually knows what they put in that stuff.

"Bread's over there. Just help yourself. This ain't no hotel," James adds. I start to wonder how James and Frankie get along. Is James this bossy with him? And is it a coincidence that he's not here to clean out that disaster of a shed?

I make two sandwiches. He doesn't object, just pours us each a cup of tea and sits down at the table. Guess he doesn't know that kids drink milk or pop. Can't fault him for that. He never had any kids of his own. Before we finish lunch, the phone rings. While James goes into the next room to answer it,

I gather up the dirty dishes. Squeezing some dish soap in the sink, I start running hot water. James isn't saying a whole lot, mostly listening to the person on the other end. Not that I'm purposely listening. It's impossible not to hear. The receiver clatters as he hangs up. I put the clean plates in the rack. James appears in the doorway. He's giving me a look and for an instant I wonder if there's something he wants to say. I dry my hands and give a nod.

"Come on, Betty Crocker," he says. "It's time to get back to work."

CHAPTER 27

FOR THE THIRD TIME THIS AFTERNOON JAMES TELLS me to get the lead out. What happened to the friendly old guy who drove out to the camp to get me? He didn't strike me as someone who'd order people around. He's not exactly cranky. Just seems that he's on a power trip or something. Not that he's a super farmer himself. He mostly stands back and watches while I do all the physical stuff, which I'm okay with, really. I'm pretty sure it would do him in, what with his breathing problems and age. I'm fourteen and he's close to a hundred and fourteen. I wouldn't want him to croak and have that on my conscience.

"Be good once we get this all organized," he says as I head toward the barn with a bag of old rope he insisted would come in handy one day. We? I want to laugh out loud.

Slowly but surely, the shed is getting organized. Not bad, considering how it looked when I started. I sure hope James appreciates my hard work, even if he is being bossy.

Speaking of James, he looks pretty comfortable sitting on a block of wood with his legs crossed, smoking a cigarette. About midafternoon I suggest we stop for a break, not that James looks like he needs one. My back hurts and my muscles are tired, but I'm not going to share that. This is still better than hanging out at some squirrel-infested shack in the middle of nowhere. James heads for the house to get me a snack, telling me to take a puff. I collapse onto the grass.

Chickens cluck in the distance and, in the field behind me, a cow makes a weird sound.

After I get my body fuelled, James hands me a shovel and says it's time to clean out the stables in the barn.

"Aren't there cows in there?"

"All out in the pasture for the day," he says, which I'm glad about. I saw their horns when we drove up this morning. They could do serious damage.

I'm aware of James watching my moves as the cow crap goes flying out the shutter. The stench is out of this world. Can't get any closer to farming than this.

Once the barn is clean, James tells me to throw sawdust in the stalls and the gutter. I don't ask the reason for the sawdust. His answer probably wouldn't make sense anyway.

"How about some nourishment?" says James when I'm about through. He doesn't have to ask again. It's the first good thing he said all afternoon. He turns and starts for the house. Standing the shovel in the corner, I hurry to catch up, wondering what's on the menu.

Butch looks up when we enter the kitchen. I take the initiative and grab the broom while James heads for the fridge. I straighten a few things up for good measure too.

The old guy actually makes a decent dinner for us, only he calls it supper—pork chops, peas and carrots, and mashed potatoes with plenty of gravy.

Afterward, I clear the table and wash the dishes while he settles in front of the TV. It's the least I can do. As I'm drying the plates, I hear him talking to the TV, grumbling over something he doesn't agree with. It's been a long day and I'm tired. I can hardly wait for my head to hit the pillow. James told me to make myself comfortable on the kitchen cot earlier. I take out my notebook and settle down.

"You coming out to watch a little TV with me? I could use the company." I sigh and put the notebook away. We just spent the whole day together. Despite James's own rudeness, I don't want to seem impolite. He really is doing me a favour here. But I've still got to come up with a game plan, some idea as to where I go from here. I can't stay with James for long. Sooner or later, someone will ask questions, like: why aren't you in school? Who are your parents?

"Tired?" James asks as I take a seat in one of the recliners.

"A bit," I say, wondering if I should admit it. When the news is over, James announces that it's time to bring in the cows. Bring in the cows? As wiped out as I am, this I've got to see.

⸻

James uses a can with *Stag Chewing Tobacco* written on it to measure out some food for the cows. We dump some in each of the mangers. Then he opens the back door and calls for the cows to come in. I stand back, waiting for a stampede that doesn't come. He keeps calling, but nothing happens. I wonder how long he'll keep this up. Those cows aren't going to come. They're free, and that's where they want to be. Besides, how smart can a cow be?

James is building some serious momentum with his "Come boss...come boss," almost chanting. But then I see movement near the trees, and here they come. James continues calling, and then the cows break out in a trot. Blows my mind. Who knew a cow would actually come running? James steps aside and they come in through the back door and straight into their stalls. They know right where they're going. Amazing. Heads down, munching on the food, James shows me how to chain them fast. When we're through, and the door is closed for the night, I look over at James. He wants to know why I'm smiling.

"The cow whisperer," I say, impressed, but James is having none of it. He gestures for me to come along.

"You gonna stand there gawking or are you coming in to watch the tube with me?" he says, turning toward the stable door. He sounds all tough, but I can tell he's smiling.

Back in the house, James flicks through the channels until he finds something he wants to watch—an old show that first aired in the nineties about a scientist who time travels by leaping into other people's bodies, fixing what went wrong in their lives, and giving them a happy ending before leaping off into someone else. Halfway through the show, my mind zones out. What if the dude from the show actually made the leap into Dad's body? Would he end up stuck there because there is no happy ending for someone with ALS?

I sit with James for a while but finally tell him I'm heading off to bed. I'm beat.

"Suit yourself," says James, reaching for the remote.

The cot is a bit lumpy, but I settle down and take out my notebook. I start thinking about home, and about Dad and Mom, as I put my pen to the page. The words come easy.

Think about living in a body that's dying from the outside in. Being imprisoned in a place so small you only have room to move your eyelids. You can barely move your hand. There are things you want to do or say, but can't. Think about living like this day in, day out. Alone inside an empty shell. Maybe you suddenly leaped into this body you know nothing about. You're a time traveller who has lost the ability to leap out. You're stuck.

Think about the meaning of your life.

Don't think about it.

You juggle these two options back and forth—day in, day out. They are the only two options you have.

Think about your brain being the only thing that works properly. A ventilator could end up being your best friend. That's if you allow it. Think about not wanting to think, because all you've got going for you are the thoughts in your head because you're trapped inside this body that doesn't want to live anymore.

If your body's dead then your brain should be too.

If there were rules for dying, that should be number one.

Live brain. Dead body. Makes no sense.

It's not my reality. It's Dad's. Yet I think about it.

No, I take that back. It's my reality, too. When something happens in a family it happens to them all. These are the things I think about.

It's not like I can tell anyone what *my* thoughts are. I have my notebook for that. Talking about this would make me look too weird, too weak. I have to be strong. It's what people expect, what my parents need. No one wants to hear what really goes on in my mind when they ask how I'm doing.

CHAPTER 28

I WAKE THROUGH THE NIGHT. BUTCH IS MAKING these weird sounds. For a time, I lie on the cot and listen. I got used to strange sounds coming from Dad's room, trying to figure out if any of those noises were not-so-good, and when or if it was something to investigate. When Butch makes a super-weird sound, I reach up and turn on the light. He's curled into a tight ball in his basket. I whisper his name, but he doesn't move. Leaning over the cot, I brush the top of his head. He squeezes his eyes and groans. I take it to mean he wants to be left alone, so I turn out the light and lie back down. Butch goes back to snoring.

In the morning, Butch lifts his head when James hobbles into the kitchen.

"Rise and shine," says James. I'm not sure if he's talking to me or Butch. He cubes up small pieces of bread, pours milk over it, and sets it on the floor. Butch creeps out of the basket and toward his dish. It's painful to watch.

"You got creaky joints too, don't ya, boy?" James pats Butch's head. "Ain't as young as you once were. Are ya, boy?" Butch sniffs his dish and starts licking at the milk.

James seems satisfied, but I'm not so sure.

"Is he okay? He was making these noises last night."

"Don't worry about old Butch. He's like me, tough as nails. Aren't ya, boy?" James continues to pat the dog's head. "There's a bowl on the counter." He opens the fridge door.

"You can gather the eggs. And leave the door open when you're done."

"The door?" I shoot him a strange look.

"The henhouse door. What door did you think I meant?" I go for the bowl.

"Well, the henhouse door, obviously," I say. Leave the henhouse door open, is he for real? Won't they run away? Seriously, I thought chickens lived in coops. "Henhouse" makes me think of a miniature house complete with a front porch, just like James's.

"They like to eat bugs," he adds.

"Whatever you say, James." Bugs? Gross. I head outside while James starts breakfast. I can't ask how to do something as simple as gathering eggs. A little kid could do that, and they actually do, only it's called an Easter egg hunt. I walk toward the henhouse. James said to leave the door open. The eggs must be in there. Good thing I figured that part out. I'd have been looking all over the place. I saw some chickens out pecking in the dirt yesterday. I thought they'd lay their eggs on the ground. Guess I was wrong.

I open the door to the henhouse and suddenly it's all feathers and squawks. I yelp and jump aside seconds before a stampede of chickens runs me over. I'm starting to think all feathered creatures are weird. First the birds back at the camp and now these nutso hens. They must like the outdoors the way they're racing to get out. Once the danger has passed and I can step inside, I get the whole reason they ran out; the smell is disgusting. I am *not* cut out for this farming stuff. Give me a hockey stick or Xbox any day. But then I remind myself that this is still better than Lenny's old camp. Food's not bad, either.

When the dust and feathers settle, I start looking around for eggs.

I check out the floor but there are no eggs there, not even one. There's water and some kind of grain sitting in dishes; lots of wood shavings and gobs of chicken turds everywhere. I check my sneakers to make sure I didn't step in any. That's when I notice the wooden nests on one of the walls. A no-brainer now that I think about it—it's like in all those Golden Books Mom used to read to me.

I start gathering the eggs, watching my step as I go. Three eggs in one nest, two in another, it's actually kind of neat the way they're lying there on top of the hay just waiting to be picked up. I go to the next nest. Empty...empty...Finding another egg, I work my way along, until I come to the last nest in the corner. The angle of how it's built makes it dark and hard to see into. I reach inside. There's something warm and furry in there. Yelling, I pull my hand back. I take a closer look.

What the...? Two round beady yellow eyes stare out at me, glowing, almost. Pulsing. It's like something from a sci-fi movie.

Creepy.

Some seriously strange sounds are coming from in there, like nothing I've ever heard.

I lean in for a closer look. Then pull back.

Dumbass—that's a hen. As in, this is a *henhouse*. Sometimes I'm surprised by my own stupidity. What else would be in a henhouse? Sheesh!

When I reach in to see if there are any eggs, she quickly shifts speed, making these even weirder sounds. I yank my hand back.

"Would you stop it, already?" She flattens down further into the hay. She's not going anywhere. But I've got to get the egg. It's a matter of principle. James would know what to do. I try shooing her away, but I don't want to piss her off either. That sends her into high gear, making even more bizarre, psycho-hen sounds. I hope hens don't have teeth. I'm pretty sure they don't.

I shove my hand in again. I'm not fast enough and she pecks me, hard.

"Knock it off," I tell her, checking out my hand. The skin is broken and there's a small bruise. No teeth, but a killer beak. It hurts like mad. I blow on the wound, give my hand a quick shake, and take a deep breath. No way is some stupid hen going to beat me. I start moving my hand in front of her like I saw in a movie one time. Only that dude was charming a snake, not a chicken. When she makes a drive toward my hand, I zoom in underneath her. Quickly locating the egg, I wrap my hand around it and yank it out. Psycho hen gets in some mad pecks, but she's too late. The egg is in the bowl. Only that's not the end of it. She moves toward me with this crazed look in her eyes, stepping out onto the edge of the nest. She's coming to get me. I slowly back up. This situation calls for calm.

"Settle down," I tell her. "Just settle down." I hold out my hand to protect my face from being pecked and clawed in case she decides to attack. I keep backing up as she positions herself on the edge of the nest. Her feet shift, and she struggles to remain balanced. She turns her head to one side and makes another strange noise. By this time, I'm totally freaked out. No way am I turning my back on this chick.

She's readying herself for takeoff. I'm frozen. Can't move. Squeezing my eyes shut, I wait to be pulverized on the spot, my face clawed to pieces.

Wait. Waiting. Any moment now.

There's a thump near my feet. My eyes snap open. She's on the floor. Now what do I do? She fluffs up her feathers, making herself bigger. Looks like she's going to explode. She keeps making weird noises.

"Nice hen," I say, moving out of her way. She makes a quick squawk, her wings flapping, then races for the open door.

She's out.

I take a deep breath. Talk about close calls. Once outside, she runs off, squawking, wings still spread wide.

I take the bowl of eggs and hurry toward the house. I check the soles of my sneakers again.

Stupid hen.

James is hanging up the phone when I step into the kitchen. He swings around and tells me to set the eggs on the counter, then starts dishing up breakfast—bacon, toast, and hash browns. I don't mention my run-in with the psycho hen. He'd only make fun.

I dive into the food. Not bad. Once breakfast is over and the dishes are done, he hustles me out the door. We leave Butch lying on the cot, sleeping. Probably couldn't stand the excitement and dozed off once his stomach was full. He seems unenergetic. But then, he's old. Rosie was a ball of energy, always on the go.

"Time to split some wood," James cackles as we step down off the doorstep. Shovelling cow turds yesterday was bad enough; I sure hope he doesn't expect me to swing an axe. I saw it once in a movie, dude had sweat running down his back. It looked hard.

"This way," he says, hobbling along. Behind the henhouse are big pieces of wood heaped into piles. Looks like enough wood for the whole neighbourhood.

"I'll warm up old Bessie," he says.

"Bessie? Isn't that, like, a cow's name?" I'm kind of proud of my knowledge.

James laughs and says, "Could be...but not this time."

He pulls away a tarp, revealing some kind of equipment.

"You seen one of these before?" he asks. I smile, pretending I know what it is.

"It's been a while. Could you do a demo?" Maybe, if he shows me, I'll catch on without looking like a dummy.

"You'll have the most important job. You get to put the junks of wood on the table—like this," he says, showing me where to place it. Junks of wood? "Once it's split—that's my job—just throw the wood over there." I look at him and nod. Sounds doable.

"No problem," I say. I'm pretty sure I can handle this. James hands me some earmuffs and tells me to put them on. These I'm familiar with; I use them when I mow the lawn.

"Gotta protect the old ears." Grinning, he puts his own earmuffs in place and starts the motor. "All set?" he says over the sound of the engine. Nodding, I go for the first piece of wood.

Turns out the most important job is also the hardest. All this wood lifting and throwing is killing my back. Some of the wood pieces weigh a ton. I can barely get the big ones up on the table for James to split. No wonder Frankie's been making himself scarce. That's if this Frankie exists, which I'm beginning to doubt. Maybe James doesn't like admitting he's got no one. Mom was friends with an old woman, Mrs. Lawrence. She used to talk about her kids all the time, what they were doing, places they travelled to. But then she died and Mom found out she didn't have any family—no kids, nothing. She'd made it all up.

"She didn't want people feeling sorry for her," Mom said. Maybe it's the same thing with James and this Frankie guy.

While I'm sweating bullets, handling the heavy pieces of wood, James is sitting all comfy in a chair pulling levers. It's noisy and sweaty and James keeps pushing me to do more.

This time we don't stop for a snack, just long enough to have what he calls a "pull of water."

"We won't worry about stacking it just yet," says James, tipping a water bottle to his lips. "That's Frankie's job anyway. We don't want to ruffle Frankie's feathers." He chuckles. He talks like Frankie's the boss. "See that pile over there? That's one of Frankie's." Okay, so it's perfect, not a piece out of place. Maybe Frankie *is* real. I can't see James stacking wood that neatly. This Frankie must be some kind of neat freak. He's probably been doing it for ages. James better not expect me to stack wood like that. Besides, Frankie's the so-called expert around here.

It's like this the whole day, me doing all the hard work while James takes it easy. Of course, he has bad knees and lungs and he's old as dirt and I'm young—sure, maybe too young to be working this hard, but I can't complain. So, I don't.

On my way to get the next piece of wood, I almost twist an ankle. I pick up a small puck-sized piece of wood and look over at James. "What's this?" I ask, mouthing the words.

"Leftovers," James yells out over the sputter of the wood splitter. "Throw it in there." He points to a white plastic bucket with *Sunspun* written across it. I see a few more pieces of wood, hidden beneath the sawdust, and throw them in.

"Nothing goes to waste," says James, cutting the motor.

Supper is steak and mushrooms, an ocean of gravy over my potatoes, and canned peas. I devour it in record time, flake out on the cot while James does the dishes. I should help the old guy, but seriously, when he told me to take a breather after we ate, I wasn't about to argue. He rouses me when it's time to call in the cows and I drag myself outside. Again, they come running when James calls. I shake my head. Remarkable.

I'm too tired to write in my notebook before bed, but promise myself I'll make up for it tomorrow. That's if I'm not zonked out again. As I'm dozing off, I hear James somewhere, I think talking on the phone. If he's not on the phone, then the old guy talks to himself. Maybe the TV again. That thought makes me smile as I pull the blanket over myself.

Butch wakes me through the night, making weird noises again. I decided it's normal for him—even Rosie would snore—and roll over. As I'm about to drift off, I start wondering how Dad's doing. I sit up. I haven't thought about home for a whole twenty-four–hour period. A record. It's always on my mind. I flop back down on the cot as guilt grabs hold of me. How could I let myself forget?

———

The next few days we work at the firewood. Not that I want to admit it, but it feels good to see our progress. I start wondering what else James will need help with. There's been no mention of him paying me, and I'm not about to bring it up. When I think back to that morning at the camp when he came out to get me, I can't recall there being any mention of money. Maybe a place to sleep and some warm meals are his idea of payment, which I'm cool with.

Toward the end of the week, I start thinking it might be time for me to leave. Someone will start wondering why I'm hanging out at James's. News travels fast. But he's kept me so busy I haven't been able to make plans. If I leave here, where will I go?

When I come in from gathering the eggs, I overhear James on the kitchen phone. His back is to the door and he doesn't see me come in.

"I told you it's temporary. A few more days, tops. He'll be crying to leave...Because I know." He laughs. "Yup...yup... good kid...the best. Okay. I'll let you know." Turning to hang up the phone, he sees me standing there. He's wearing this sheepish grin. Awkward. We both know he was talking about me. Really? I've become the gossip in these parts. I hand him the eggs and go shower before breakfast.

I'll be crying to leave? Is that what this has been about, James pushing me so I'll get pissed and take off? He pours coffee for the two of us, then motions for me to sit. I should pack my things and go. I'm a laughingstock as far as James is concerned. Except the food smells good and I'm super hungry, not to mention I haven't yet come up with a decent plan for myself.

"By the way, I've asked Frankie to come give us a hand today," announces James.

Frankie. Great. I bet that's who James was talking to earlier on the phone. Nice that he was laughing about me with this Frankie guy, probably telling him I'm good for nothing.

"Kinda looking to finish splitting the wood today. Things'll pick up once Frankie gets here," James says halfway through our meal. He looks confident, which is highly annoying. That's all I've heard all week long. Every time I'm doing something, it's Frankie this and Frankie that. What's so great about Frankie? What's he got that I don't? Can't James see I've been giving it my all? What does the old guy expect? I've been working my butt off, but obviously that's not good enough.

He needs Frankie. Not only that, I'm basically working for free. I wonder what he pays Frankie.

"You'll learn a lot from Frankie," says James, smiling.

That's it. I've had it with all this Frankie talk. I put down my fork. "Oh yeah?" I say, cutting him off before he can say anything else. "Where's he been all this time while I've been here sweating my butt off?" James keeps eating. It's like he hasn't heard what I've said, and it's really pissing me off. I start picking up the corners of the placemats.

"You looking for something?" James seems confused. Good. I've finally got his attention.

"I'm looking for Frankie," I say. "Only I don't see him. You know why? Because I'm here and he isn't, that's why."

James takes a sip of his coffee. He looks me straight in the eye. "I told you back at the camp that Frankie was busy. That's why I came out to get you."

Oh right, he did say that. I keep my head down, stab at the scrambled eggs on my plate. Now I'm just an idiot.

We finish eating in silence. I was acting like a jerk and now I've gone and pissed James off. He'll kick me out, maybe drop me off back at the camp. Why didn't I keep my big mouth shut? We do the dishes and head outside. Talk about awkward. I know I've got to say something. Smooth things over between us. But what? I search for something to say, anything.

"So, tell me, what's so great about Frankie? You never did say," I ask as we walk toward the woodpile. It's all I've got.

Scowling, James says, "You jealous of Frankie or something?"

"Jealous? Who, me? Pfff." I keep walking along, playing it cool, but I'm so happy he's talking to me. He may as well have said, "You just won a million dollars." From now on I'll watch what I say. This might be an okay day after all. I'm actually a little curious about Frankie. "Seriously, what's the deal with him, James?"

James looks over and gives this goofy grin. "You'll see."

I pick up a piece of wood. "What kind of answer is that? Is it a big secret?"

"You'll see," he repeats, smiling bigger this time. Was that a twinkle I saw in his eye?

"Seriously, what's he got, muscles on top of muscles? Or maybe he's superhuman? Is that it, does he have super-powers? Does his crap have muscles?" I ask, jokingly. By now I've decided no matter what, I'm not going to hold anything against Frankie. I'll make sure we get along. Besides, he'll be making my job easier. Or at least I hope so.

James's refusal to answer piques my curiosity even more. He starts up the wood splitter. We're just getting started when an SUV rolls into the yard. When James sees the vehicle, he cuts the motor. The SUV comes to a stop. The passenger side door opens. I look over at James.

All right. I *am* an idiot.

CHAPTER 29

A GIRL CLIMBS OUT OF THE PASSENGER'S SIDE. SHE'S wearing coveralls and a ball cap. I'd guess she's in her late teens.

She waves at James. "I'm here. Finally." She seems pretty happy. She stops, looks at me, then looks back at James. "You didn't say someone was going to help us."

"What's this, I have to run everything past you first?" jokes James.

"Who are you?" she says.

"Sa—" I stop. What am I thinking? "Jack, my name's Jack." She thinks for a few moments.

"Like Jack be nimble?" She smiles, like she's surprised she made the connection.

"Not quite," I tell her and glance over at James. He looks amused.

A woman steps out of the driver's side of the SUV and walks toward James. She's smiling.

"Frankie was going to walk if I didn't soon bring her," she says. "Such impatience."

"She's a big help around here. Couldn't run the farm without her. You get to depend on people."

The woman looks at me.

"That there's Jack," says James. "Picked him up the other day on the number ten. Not doing too bad. Can't take Frankie's place though. No one could do that." He pauses. "Jack...this here's Betty. She brings Frankie out to the farm once a week to help out."

"They make a good team," says Betty, smiling. "Frankie keeps James in his place." I smile. That, I wouldn't mind seeing.

"I'll be back the usual time," Betty says. "If something comes up, give me a call." James nods. He pulls out a pouch of roll-your-owns and twists up a cigarette as Betty gets in her SUV and drives off.

Frankie doesn't waste any time, heads on over to the pile of split wood like she's done it a hundred times before. Pulling a pair of gloves out of her back pocket, she starts stacking the wood. She doesn't have to ask what to do. She just knows. I'm staring, and I know it. She sees me watching her.

"What?" she says. "Surprised that I'm a girl or that I have Down syndrome? Now get over here and help me." She gestures for me to come over.

"First, you put down skids," she says, laying some poles on the ground. I can tell she's done this before. She begins meticulously piling the split wood onto the skids.

"You've got to do it right or the pile will fall over," she says, showing me the proper way.

Frankie doesn't stop. I'm in awe of the way she knows exactly what she's doing, mainly because I've had to figure everything out—and apparently, I went pretty slow, given how fast she's going at it. She's like a wood-stacker extraordinaire. No wonder James likes having her around.

"Get back to work, lazy bones," scolds Frankie, looking over at James. Her brow is knit. This girl is serious.

"Hold your britches," he says, taking his sweet old time to light the cigarette. I look over at James and we grin. He starts up the wood splitter and I go for a block of wood.

Midmorning, James shuts things down and sends Frankie into the house to get drinks. He's almost through gassing up the wood splitter when the screen door slams. Frankie starts waving her arms. Alarmed, he hands me the gas jug and heads toward the house, Frankie yelling like the house is on fire.

"It's Butch!"

I sit the jug down and hurry behind James. I could easily pass him, but don't. Butch is his dog. It wouldn't be right for me to barge on ahead.

By the time James reaches the house, he's breathing weird, but he pushes on. Butch's basket is empty. He's crawled out and is trying to make it onto the cot. Only he doesn't have the strength in him. He whines. Frankie starts brushing Butch and telling him he's a good boy. Butch doesn't pay much attention to her. It's like he's zoned out, maybe in another world. He's determined to make it onto the cot.

"It's time I take old Butch to the vet," says James, helping him up. I can tell Butch is in a lot of pain.

"I want to go with you and Butch," says Frankie.

"Sorry, kid," says James. "You'll have to sit this one out. I need you to hold down the fort."

Frankie groans. "But James. That's not fair. Butch is my buddy, too."

For the first time there's a genuine look of concern on James's face. "You stay here with Jack and work at the wood. Your mother will be coming by at four." James is right. It might be for the best. There's nothing Frankie can do to help Butch. And I'm obviously not the best wood-stacker around. I don't have the experience that Frankie does. James won't be too happy with me if the wood falls over. Piling wood sounds a lot easier than it is. Besides all that, I don't want to be left here alone.

"I thought he'd have more time," says James. Looking down at Butch, he pats the dog's head, then gathers him up in a blanket.

More time? I look at Frankie. What's James talking about?

"He's just sick," I say, brushing Butch's head. "The vet can fix it."

"That's right, the vet will make him better," agrees Frankie.

"Not this time."

"Why not wait to see what the vet has to say? There could be some medicine." I hate that he sounds defeatist.

James is shaking his head. "I knew it was coming. Vet only gave him a few months. It's been nearly a year now. You showed her, didn't you boy?" He lays his hand on Butch's head. It takes a while for me to digest what James is saying. I don't really know Butch, but this news feels like a punch in the gut.

I glance over at James. He looks like he's lost his best friend.

CHAPTER 30

I OPEN THE PASSENGER SIDE DOOR FOR JAMES. HE gently lays Butch on the truck seat. Butch yelps a couple of times but quiets once James gets him settled. He covers him with a small blanket and touches the top of his head. Butch closes his eyes. Frankie stands in the background, wringing her hands, saying, "Poor old Butch...poor old Butch."

"Last call, old boy," says James looking down at his best friend. "Time to head over that rainbow bridge they all talk about. I hear it's a nice spot." Pausing, he looks down at Butch before closing the door. I look across at Frankie, swallow the lump in my throat.

Seeing James and Butch drive off is like Rosie all over again. Me sitting in the Jeep beside Dad holding her on my lap, knowing what the outcome was going to be. The sound of the rifle fire, Rosie's piercing cry. The very last day, the last frigging hour. What were the chances? We would have been on our way home if Rosie hadn't seen the deer and taken off after it. Four years, and it's hard not to think that it was my fault. If only I hadn't let her run down to the lake that one last time. It was a Sunday morning. No hunting on Sundays. At least that's how it's supposed to be.

James pulls out onto the road and Frankie yanks on my arm.

"Work time," she says, snapping me back to reality. "We're holding down the fort—remember? I'll show you how to pile the wood again. James wants us to keep working."

I smile. James is right. Frankie sure is a worker.

Still holding tight to my arm, she leads me back to the pile of wood. Honestly, I'm glad for the distraction.

Stacking wood isn't as easy as it looks. I keep trying to get it right. Frankie's got loads of patience and that's probably a good thing. She doesn't get mad when the wood I'm piling starts to lean. Instead, she helps straighten it so it won't fall over. Insisting there's a right way to do it, she shows me again.

When I find some small round pieces of wood under the sawdust, we start kicking them back and forth, kind of like stick handling, only we don't have hockey sticks and the round pieces of wood aren't pucks.

"You're good," says Frankie when one shoots through her feet. I sit on a big block of wood, taking a breather while Frankie takes James's chair for herself. I tell her I used to play hockey.

"Hockey?" She looks like she's considering it.

"In my other life, that is."

"Your other life?" Frankie looks as though she's considering that, too. "So, why don't you play in this life?"

I grab up the round pieces of wood and toss them in the Sunspun bucket, then shrug. "I gave it up."

Frankie looks at me. "Well, do you like hockey?"

"Like it? Hockey's my thing—at least it *was* my thing. You don't just stop liking something you're good at."

"If you're good at it and you like it, then why would you give it up? That doesn't make sense."

I'm not sure how to answer that. It's too complicated. "Time we got back to work," I tell her. "James could come home anytime."

"Anytime," says Frankie, snapping her head in agreement. "He'll say we're goofing off."

Why did I go and bring all *that* up? Makes me miss hockey all over again. Hockey is gone, and I won't be getting it back. I thought I'd faced that fact.

We go back to stacking the wood.

When lunchtime rolls around, we make sandwiches. I pour us each a pop. Feels weird without James here, even weirder with Butch's empty basket in the kitchen.

We talk about all sorts of things. I don't know why, but I admit to her that I'm really just a city kid.

"That explains a lot," she says, and we both laugh.

Turns out she met James through a community program that pairs volunteers up with seniors like James who need help doing their work. I catch myself wondering if there's a program like that in the city. It's something I could get behind. Helping James hasn't been all bad. I actually don't mind hanging out with seniors. But then I stop myself. I don't live there anymore. There won't be any programs for me. Not only that, I can't stay here with James much longer either.

"Why did you pick James?" I ask, biting into my sandwich.

"Simple," she says. "I like working outdoors...and I like the animals...and I didn't want to clean anyone's house." I bite into my sandwich. Frankie's right on all counts.

Leaving here is going to be hard.

The afternoon goes along well and we get a lot accomplished. Probably not as much as James would have liked, but something tells me he'll be satisfied. Frankie's good company. No wonder James likes having her around.

When James gets back home from the vet's, he carries Butch's blanket into the house, but no Butch. We keep stacking the wood.

"If he wants to talk, he'll come to us," says Frankie.

James stays in the house for what seems like a very long time. Probably making himself a bite to eat. He did miss lunch. He finally hobbles down off the steps and makes his way toward us. Looking at our piles of wood, he shakes his head, smiling.

"Not bad," he says. His eyes are glassy, but he doesn't mention Butch. Not that I have to ask. I already know. No need to hear details.

"You can have the fort back," Frankie tells James. He doesn't say anything, just starts up the wood splitter.

CHAPTER 31

BETTY DRIVES IN AT FOUR O'CLOCK. FROM THE PAS-
senger's seat, Frankie waves, and then just like that she's gone.
Suddenly, everything feels empty. James had wanted to finish
splitting the wood today, but the universe had other plans. Life
has a way of shifting in an instant. I think about Dad. One day
he was using a walker, the next he was in a wheelchair, then
waiting for a hospital bed to arrive at the house.

"Time to head on in," says James. I think we both feel
empty.

Back in the house, James places the blanket in Butch's basket and sets it out on the porch—out of sight, out of mind. I
want to ask if he's okay, but he probably doesn't want to talk.
Talking is way overrated. Besides, guys from James's gener-
ation don't talk about their feelings. They stuff it down, pretending there's nothing wrong. You can ask Grandpa Gillis—if
he were alive, that is.

It's nearing dinnertime. Despite looking defeated, James
starts putting some food together. Maybe I should offer to
help. The kitchen feels weird without Butch, like all the air
has been sucked out of the room. I glance down and see his
empty dishes by the cot. I thought James might have moved
them by now. He's cubing up small bits of bread the way he
does before every meal. I'm not sure what to do—leave him
alone or remind him he doesn't have to do that anymore?

I can't just sit here and watch James cube Butch's bread. At some point it's going to click, and I don't want to be there to witness that. I make my way out to the porch, stand looking out at the road. Not much for traffic this time of day, but I'm getting used to the quiet here.

I'm pretty sure I know how James feels. The days after Rosie was gone were the loneliest times of my life. Everywhere I went, there were reminders. All this makes me wonder how our house will be once Dad's no longer there. I take a breath, remind myself that I'm not going there. I'll remember the good times and that's it, think about Dad before ALS. These past few days, I've managed to keep some of that bad crap out of my head, and that's exactly what I plan to keep doing.

Again, I hear James talking on the phone. Can't make out what's he's saying. Probably letting someone know that Butch is gone. There must be people he wants to tell. This really sucks. Now he has no one. I'd been planning to take off soon. I've been here too long already, and he's going to start wondering what my real story is. What will I tell him? I'm pretty sure he knows I should be in school; he's not that out of it. I can't believe he hasn't asked already. Almost a whole week and nothing. I finally decide he doesn't really give a crap about my education, or lack of, so long as he gets his wood split and piled. I'm probably stronger than Frankie, even though I'm not as good yet, and he saw my being here as an opportunity. Who could blame him?

The cows out in the pasture start mooing, long and drawn out. They're crying, or at least it sounds like it. Do they sense what's going on with James? He *is* the cow whisperer, after all.

Weird as it sounds, I feel safe here with the cows and even the psycho hens. Maybe I *can* stay, fly under the radar. James might keep quiet if he needs my help, and now with Butch gone, he'll be lonely. The other night, he mentioned that he only had grade nine, so maybe he won't care if I go to school. But there's Frankie. Is there enough work for the two of us? I mull all these things over. Then I wonder how long I can stand it without internet, without actually getting an education? There's still a lot out there that I'm curious about. What I discovered with Dad being sick is that I like doing research. Going a week without being online, without a keyboard, is one thing, but forever? And my notebook will be full soon. Then what? I kick at the floorboards. It sounds like I'm trying to cash in on Butch's death when that's the furthest thing from my mind.

After a time, James joins me out on the porch. He doesn't say anything, just stands there. I sense him beside me, hear him breathing. He reeks of cigarette smoke. I can't think of a thing to say. I only just met Butch a few days back and now he's gone. Poor old Butch. I could tell James about Rosie, let him know that I kind of understand how he's feeling. But I'm not going to make this about me. No one wants you diminishing their pain by telling them *your* story. In the beginning, people would do that when they heard about Dad's illness. Honestly, when that diagnosis comes, you're being handed a death sentence. So many people claimed to know. There was always someone they knew of or heard tell of who had ALS, all of them in worse shape than Dad. He should feel grateful when they pointed that out to him because he was still able to walk at that time.

James slaps me on the shoulder, says it's time to go in and eat. Once we're sitting at the table, he starts unloading.

"He was a good old dog. Not many like old Butch. Faithful. We had some good times over the years."

"I bet you did." I swallow a gulp of milk. James pauses and I get the feeling he's reliving some of those good times.

"He wasn't a pup when I got him, you know." He looks at me with a raised eyebrow. "Some old widow didn't want to be bothered with him after her husband died. Dropped dead in the dooryard, he did. Saw the advertisement in the paper. *One dog to give away, mixed breed, some beagle. A year old. House broken.* I called, thinking that dog would be gone for sure. Things don't last long once they're in the paper. I thought, why not go take a look? Didn't figure I'd take him. Dogs are a lot of work."

No kidding. Rosie was constantly running off. I try to picture James hurrying after an energetic Butch.

James bites into a piece of bread and starts chewing. "So, I made arrangements to go look at him. 'There's someone else coming at two,' she said. 'They sounded quite interested,' she said. 'Better hurry up.'"

James stops talking. He looks up at me and grins. "She had me then. Wasn't going to let someone else get their hooks in him before I even laid eyes on him—no sir." He chuckles and eats a few bites. He stops and looks back up at me, shaking his head. "And then the fun started."

I don't say much, just let him talk. He starts telling me about Butch's illness—some weird thing with his pancreas, the trips to the vet, the money spent, which he says was worth every penny.

"Why didn't you tell me?" I might have done something differently. I could have given him the VIP treatment.

"Wasn't expecting it to come on like this. Thought you'd be long gone. But," he says, gathering up the dirty dishes, "he lasted longer than they said he would." He seems satisfied, proud to think that Butch defied what the experts had to say. I get that. Once again, I consider telling him about Rosie.

"Stayed with him to the end. It didn't take long after they gave him the needle." He pauses, then starts talking again. "I can pick him up in a few weeks, they told me. There's a pet cemetery not far from there. That's where I'll take his ashes when the time is right. I've had me a lot of dogs over the years. Butch was tops."

We wash the dishes and bring in the cows like it's an ordinary evening. Afterward, James asks if I want to watch some TV with him. I tell him I'm good but then change my mind after seeing the look on his face. Of course he wants company. Why wouldn't he? He turns on an old game show, buddy playing to win a million dollars.

"Now, what's *he* going to do with a million bucks?" says James, pointing at the screen. "Look at him." The guy must be at least eighty. "Give it to some young person that needs it."

"Sounds good," I say, smiling. A million dollars—that would solve all my problems. I could buy a house. I wouldn't even have to work.

Later, alone in the kitchen, I take out my notebook and start writing. Butch dying has me thinking about Rosie again.

CHAPTER 32

ROSIE LOVED RUNNING. WHEN SHE WAS A PUPPY, OUR *backyard gave her plenty of space, but as she grew that same fence became her prison. She'd stop and look out into the street, eyes pleading. Then one day Dad came home with a leash and told me I was about to learn responsibility.*

Every day after school, I'd take her around the block. Sunshine, rain, windstorms, snowstorms, we faced it all. Rosie was a beagle; she wanted to run, to chase and be chased. To bark and run and run some more. She wanted to be free, to feel the wind against her fur, to stretch out her legs and just go, go, go!

One day Rosie broke out of her prison. We made phone calls. We searched the neighbourhood, calling her name.

"She'll come home when she gets hungry," Mom said. But I worried. What if Rosie got hit by a car or dognapped? What if she never came home—ever? What if she just disappeared without a trace? What if she...

Rosie was on the doorstep the next morning. She raced through the house like she'd never been so happy. I hugged her neck and promised to never let her go again. She licked my face, and if you think dogs can't smile you're wrong. Sometimes you don't appreciate what you have until it's gone—like that song Dad used to sing along to with the big yellow taxi in it.

Once we made it to camp that fall, Rosie was like another dog. For the first time there was nothing stopping her. She ran down to the lakeshore and sniffed along the beach, and hurried through the trails. She was unstoppable.

I stop writing and look up. I know what comes next and I don't like it. If it hadn't been for Butch and James, I might not have had the courage to go further. But it's been close to four years. It's time I faced this. I pick up my pen and turn back toward my notebook.

We took one last trip down to the lake while Dad packed up the Jeep. And then I saw it, close to the strip of trees—a deer with a big set of horns. Rosie was pawing into the sand, unaware that we were being watched. The second she caught sight of the deer she was running, straining her throat as she bayed like the hound she was. The flip of a white tail and the deer disappeared. I chased after Rosie, calling for her to come back. Then I heard the shot.

Setting aside the notebook, I take Rosie's ashes out of my backpack. I run my hand across the engraved name. Maybe I should have buried them out at the camp or down by the beach. She liked it there. Except I wasn't ready. The box makes me feel close to her.

James hobbles out into the kitchen. "Whatcha got there?" he asks, going to the fridge.

I tell him it's my dog. He doesn't ask for an explanation, just twists the top off a two-litre bottle of pop. It fizzes.

"Want some?" he asks, showing me the bottle of cream soda. I shake my head. Does anyone actually drink that stuff? He pours a glass and sits at the table. I watch him sip the pop, trying to work up the courage to tell him what's on my mind, that it's probably time for me to leave.

"Look, I've been thinking I should probably get going...I don't want to outstay my welcome." This feels more awkward than I imagined.

"I was wondering when it was going to come around to this," he says, setting his empty glass on the table. I feel like a butthole. He just lost Butch. Now he'll be all alone. Except I can't stay here forever. We both know that.

"Guess I can't keep you here against your will. Mind telling me your plans?" He chuckles.

Wish I was in on the joke. When I heard him on the phone earlier today, it sounded as though he could hardly wait for me to go. He even laughed; said I'd be begging to leave. Guess he'll be glad when I'm out of here.

"My plans?" I don't have any real plans. So much for buying a tent to live in. That'll take money and right now, I haven't got any. It would be nice if James paid me, even a little. But I have to tell him something. He doesn't even know my real name. "I haven't made up my mind. But I'm thinking of staying with my dad for a while."

He looks surprised. "Your old man? You don't say." Why is that so hard for him to believe?

"I'll probably head to Beach Meadows to stay with him and his new girlfriend. They said I could come anytime and if I like it, they said I could stay on and start school."

James nods in a knowing way. I lie back on the cot, arms behind my head. I knew he'd believe me.

"I'll probably leave tomorrow, after breakfast, if that's okay." Is it right of me to expect him to feed me before I go? I'm wondering if I should mention money or leave it at me just having a place to sleep and some hot meals for a few days. I don't want to push my luck.

"Why not stay..."

I raise up on my elbow, interested in what he's going to say. Could it be?

"...at least until after lunch tomorrow? We can finish up the wood."

The wood? Of course, the wood. Excuse me for thinking that James actually likes having me around. Guess I'm no Frankie. I lie back down and say, "Sure," in a casual way. "Does the bus come out this way?"

James laughs. "The bus? Where do you think you are? You're not in the city now."

City? "What are you talking about? I never said I was from the city." I laugh as if to say he's got it all wrong. He shoots me a look. We both know I'm lying. That didn't even sound convincing.

"Pardon me," says James. I don't think he cares one way or the other. His biggest concern is getting his wood split. I get it—I guess.

All this time, I thought I had James fooled. Clearly, he's sharper than I thought.

I lie on the cot thinking about my next step while James goes off to watch TV. Seriously, I've got nothing. Going home is out of the question, especially with what Dad's planning. I can't handle that, and if I don't know what's really going on at home, I can go on pretending that everything's fine.

The TV's loud. I'm wiped but I still can't sleep. I can't stop myself from thinking about what lies ahead. If I did have to go back home and Dad found someone else to help him, I'd lose it for sure. Call me selfish. I don't want him to suffer near the end, but another part of me wants him with us every last moment he's got. Maybe he's got more time than they think. Maybe he'll be like Stephen Hawking. Maybe he'll...

No. I'm dreaming, and I've got to stop it, stick to my original plan of never going home.

I hear James talking back to the TV again. Can't help smiling. He sounds wound up. Like anything he's saying is going to make a difference.

The phone rings. Sputtering, James goes to answer it.

"I wanna finish up the wood," I hear him say as I settle down for the night. My last night here. I fall asleep with James still mumbling in the background.

———

The morning is grey. I look out the window. Maybe rain is on the way. Great, I'll be trying to thumb a ride in the rain. Somewhere in the middle of the night, I decided hitchhiking is my only option. I considered asking James to drive me to the nearest town. Middleton, maybe. And from there, I'm not sure.

Like every other day, I go do the egg thing while James puts breakfast together.

Psycho hen is back on the nest in the corner when I walk into the henhouse, as evil-looking as ever. I won't miss her. I gather the eggs and leave her alone. I'm not messing with her today.

James chats through breakfast like it's just another day for him. He doesn't mention Butch, but maybe that's a good thing. I've heard that the sooner you can let go of your grief, the better.

"Should be able to finish up this morning," says James as we walk toward the pile of wood. It's definitely shrunk since the first day we started.

"It won't all be stacked," I say, hopefully. Maybe I can drag another day or two out of this.

"Frankie's going to help with that. Splitting's the biggest job." James turns his back and starts the wood splitter, probably for the last time while I'm here. I pick through the wood, putting a piece in place to be split. I'm going through the motions, but my heart's not in it. We push through lunch, finishing up the last few pieces. When there's nothing left but sawdust, James shuts the wood splitter down. My stomach rumbles. I'm starved. Yet James appears to be in no hurry to cook. We put the tarp back over the splitter, fastening it tight.

Lunch is leftovers from the stew he made a few days ago. I start thinking how awkward the goodbyes will be. We're finishing up the dishes when I hear a vehicle drive in. Frankie? I spin around to see. The dish towel I'm holding slips out of my hand.

No way. Can't be.

CHAPTER 33

"GONNA STAND THERE GAWKING ALL DAY?" SAYS James, wiping his hands dry. I look back at him. He's got that goofy grin on his face.

"But how?" I'm confused. This doesn't make any sense. My heart makes a wild jump. I thought I'd never see Mom again.

"You think a kid goes missing and it's not all over the news?" says James. "Nice picture, by the way. You're famous."

The news? Duh! I do a facepalm. I look over at James. He's smiling.

"So all this time you knew?" He nods and purses his lips.

"Why do you think I came back to get you, Sam?" Now I feel stupid, telling him my name was Jack when he knew all along.

"I thought you needed..." I shrug. "You know, help...with your wood."

"Oh, I needed help, there's no disputing that. And you needed time to figure things out. I thought if I worked you hard, you'd be anxious to go home."

I'm blown away. I can't wrap my head around this. At all. James chuckles.

"I was leaving today," I remind him.

"To God knows where. That song and dance you gave about Beach Meadows. Nice touch, kid."

I look at him sheepishly.

"Never met anyone quite as stubborn. You even got Frankie beat. How about that?"

Something about this still doesn't make sense. "Wait...you know my folks?" I'm still trying to piece things together.

"Not until a few days ago, and only by phone."

"You were talking to *Mom*?"

"She's been itching to come get you, but I held her off. Told her this would be good for you."

Okay, it's starting to click, but there are parts I'm still not getting here, some missing pieces. "But Mom," I say. How did she wind up here?

Mom's red Toyota comes to a stop. A weird feeling hits me. A punch to the gut. What's she going to say about the other day, me taking off like that? And Dad? He wanted my help and I failed him. Wait. Where is Dad? I left him alone last Saturday—not a smart thing to do. Please don't tell me something has happened to him. I can't imagine Mom coming out here alone.

No. It can't be.

My feet are stuck on the spot. I fight off this urge to race toward the car. My heart is beating all weird. There's thumping in my ears. Not sure I can handle the truth.

James pushes me toward the door. "What are you waiting for?" he says.

I move forward, uncertain. Mom jumps out of the car, looking like she's about to sprint toward me, but she's holding back. I stand in the doorway. We stare at each other and then she reaches out. I hurry toward her.

Her arms feel good. She's sobbing, her face buried into my shoulder.

"Sam," she whispers, and my throat makes this strange sound. We stand there all awkward until James hollers from the doorway, telling us to come on in. Mom looks at me and smiles.

I manage to pull it together. "We'd better listen to James," I say, turning toward the house. "He's kind of bossy."

James finally fills in the missing pieces of the story while we sit at the kitchen table. "Remember when you mentioned Lenny Porter?" He pours Mom some tea and I nod. "Like I told you the other day, I know Lenny. I've even dickered with him a time or two. Had this white-face steer once, and do you suppose he'd take a decent dollar for it? No, no. What he was asking for it was way over the top. He—"

"Can you get on with the story?" I say.

James looks surprised. "Sorry," he says, pausing a few moments as he tries to get back on track.

"Lenny?" I remind him.

"Right. Yeah. Lenny. So I calls him up when I sees your picture on the news and I gets some information from him. He never lends his camp out without getting phone numbers. You said you stayed there with your old man. Kind of figured that in itself would make you stand out for Lenny. And I was right." James is smiling.

He can sure stretch out a story.

"We were beside ourselves with worry," says Mom, breaking in. "Everyone was looking, the police, your friends. We hadn't even considered the camp. But then James called."

"I'd say they were worried," says James, grinning. "Every time I turned around she was calling on the phone, wanting to come get you."

It's hard to look at Mom, thinking of the pain I caused. She has way too much on her plate without me adding to it. "Sorry. I didn't mean to worry anyone." What a dumb thing to say. Why wouldn't they be worried? I was only thinking about myself.

"No, Sam. You're not to apologize. Everything with your dad has been hard on you, and we didn't recognize just *how* hard. We should have." Mom has that strained look in her eye. Please don't let her start crying. She takes a deep breath. "Can we just go home?" she says.

Home. Sounds good to me. Smiling, I look at Mom. "Best thing I've heard all week."

James takes that as his cue. He gets up from the table. "Don't forget your things," he says.

I make sure everything's in my backpack—Rosie, my note-book, clothes, iPod, the framed photo of Rosie and me—yup, all there. I straighten the wrinkles out of the bedding on the cot. I think about Butch. I haven't really said anything to James and I should.

"Sorry about old Butch. From one dog owner to another, it sucks. He was a good old boy."

James nods.

"Maybe you'll get yourself another dog one day."

"Maybe. But not likely. It would have to be a special situation, like when I found Butch."

I hate that I said that. What's wrong with me? People said that to me after Rosie was gone. It made me feel worse.

"I'm getting too old to be thinking about another dog," adds James.

"Old? Who, you?" I smile.

"All set?" says Mom, and I nod. She turns to James. "You're Sam's guardian angel. I can't thank you enough for taking care of him. I must owe you something." She opens her handbag. James is shaking his head. He's having nothing of that.

"This one here was a big help to me," he says, slapping me on the shoulder. "I should be owing him. Got my shed cleaned out and wood all split. Now, put your money away."

Mom looks at him, smiles, and closes her purse.

"Don't go making yourself a stranger, Sam. Come back anytime. There's always work needs doing," says James as he waves from the porch. Work? Leave it to James. As we turn in the yard, I can't help feeling a little sad.

"He seems nice," says Mom as we head down the driveway. She looks over at me for like the tenth time since we got in the car. She can't seem to wipe that smile off her face. I've missed seeing her smile.

"James is *okay*." I nod, thinking about all the things that happened while I was with him—gathering eggs from psycho hens, wood-splitting, cleaning out the shed, and bringing in the cows. And poor old Butch. I thought it would be rough for James, being all alone with Butch gone. But he's got Frankie, and something tells me he's going to be all right.

The drive into the city takes forever. Just getting to the highway is excruciatingly slow. Mom chit-chats all the way. I'm still waiting for the bawling out I know is coming. I took off, without telling anyone. I'm pretty sure there will be some punishment. But there are things I need to know. I feel awkward bringing it up. But it's killing me.

"Dad?" I steal a glance at Mom, to see her reaction.

"Don't worry about Dad." Her smile is comforting. "He's doing okay. He just wants you home—we both do."

"But, what about...?" Words are easier to write than to speak.

"Oh Sam, life is complicated. But nothing you should worry about."

"I thought..."

"I know what you thought when I saw the kit you left out. We both know what you thought. I talked to your dad. People change their minds, all the time. I know he's discussed certain things in the past, his personal thoughts on euthanasia. But he would *never* want you to be a part of anything like that. *Ever*." She squeezes my hand.

"But the kit came. I thought that meant he was ready...you know, to go." I glance over at Mom again then look away. "And I heard you say you couldn't do it."

"Oh Sam. You don't understand. First of all, Dad would never put that on you, and secondly, he ordered that kit three years ago. He was newly diagnosed. He thought he'd have plans in place by the time it arrived, and then only if he felt it was needed. He obviously didn't think things through. But who can blame him? He was probably still in shock, we all were."

"But three years ago?" I'm still confused. "It just arrived."

"Yes, three years ago. There are companies that do that, like you can have flowers sent to loved ones on anniversaries after you're gone...Oh Sam, he wasn't thinking back then. And then the disease, it took over. He forgot about the order he placed. We both did. But know that he never expected for you to be the one. *Never*."

"You were crying. The other day in the living room when Marcie was there."

"I hate what this disease is doing to our family, and I love your dad." She brushes some tears away and keeps talking. "And I'm probably going to cry again. More than once before this is all over. This thing with your dad has been hard on us all. Not just him."

Mom's right. The things I've had to give up, the guilt I've carried, haven't been easy, but she's given up tons too. I didn't think about what she might be feeling, only myself.

Mom looks at me, her eyes pleading. "Promise me that from now on we'll talk things through, no matter what. We'll handle this disease as it comes along. Together. Like a family. You don't have to face any of this alone. Ever again, Sam. Do you hear me?" She reaches across and touches my arm. The relief I feel is phenomenal. This is one promise I know I can keep.

We drive up to the house and the place feels weird, like I've been gone for years instead of days. Marcie comes out to meet us.

"It's about time," she says, her hands on her hips. She doesn't offer up any hugs, but I can tell she's happy to see me. Facing Dad's going to be the hard part. I stop the moment I see him in the living room. What do I say?

His eyes soften. I drop my backpack and hurry toward him.

"Welcome back," he says. But there's more—things that aren't part of his banked messages, and yet I know.

Late night, alone in my room. I take out my notebook. It's almost full.

Things change, but only if we learn to communicate on the same level. I'm finding that no matter how hard things are to talk about, hiding, pretending they don't exist doesn't help. Find some way to make yourself be heard. If you can't say it, write it.

I look down at my entry. Some lessons are harder to learn than others, but there's a satisfaction to be gained once they're learned. At the moment, I'm not sure what the end will look like. But Mom's right, whatever way it goes down, we'll face it together. The way a family should.

EPILOGUE

AUGUST 2016

DAD WANTED THINGS TO BE PRIVATE, AND YOU DO what someone wants so long as it's reasonable. For me, that was a hard lesson to learn. He's sitting in the back seat, driver's side, a seat belt around the urn that holds his ashes. Rosie is on the seat beside him. Something about that feels right.

Mom, Marcie, and I—we're not saying a whole lot, although every once in a while, Mom comments on something out the window. Marcie answers her back as if she's interested. It's not a sightseeing trip. We all know that. Mom's trying to keep things light because that's what Mom does.

We turn down Sawmill Road and park. I warned Mom not to take her car down the gravel road leading to Lenny Porter's camp before we started out today. Too many rocks and holes, not to mention the bushes.

We walk. I'm carrying the urn. It's part of what Dad wanted. Mom's chatting away. There's a new fundraiser she's involved in. Truthfully, I haven't heard this much fire in her voice since before Dad got sick. It's nice.

I don't remember the camp being this far in. Someone has recently cut the bushes along side the road and they're lying neatly piled off to the side. It's been nearly two years since I was here. Nature is constantly changing.

"So, this is it?" says Mom when we reach our destination. She sounds surprised.

"Impressive, right?" I say, sarcastically. I smile.

Mom looks around at the pine trees, the camp, the outhouse, finally toward the sky. The sun finds its way through the tangle of tree limbs and lands softly on her face. I've forgotten how pretty she is.

"Your father liked the simple things. It's why he came out here every year with his friends. It was his thing. I was surprised the year he wanted to bring you, Sam." A tear glistens in her eye. Could be the wind, but I doubt that.

Marcie's being unusually quiet. Maybe it's the tone of the whole day. "Nice spot," she says, finally speaking up. She walks around the clearing, examining the landscape. "Lots of trees."

"Glad you approve," I say. Marcie's not the outdoors type, but I'm glad she came along. She made Dad's last days comfortable. He liked her.

"A bit rustic." Mom opens the door to the camp and looks inside. I smile. That's how Dad always described it. I check around for the squirrels but don't see them. I seriously don't see anything, not even a bird. Maybe we chased them off. Mom talked most of the way in.

"We should probably get this over with," says Mom after a while. It feels like we're stalling, which we probably are. The ashes have been a part of our lives for close to six months.

Marcie stays back at the camp while Mom and I head toward the beach. Tiny waves break the water's surface. Sunlight sparkles.

"It's beautiful here. I can see now why your dad loved it," Mom says, looking out across the water. We don't go onto the sand. We stand for a while, feeling the breeze. "Might just as well make fertilizer," Dad said back when he told us what his wishes were. A real joker, my dad. Mom removes the top of the urn and together we release the ashes. The wind scatters them across the grass. I look at Mom and smile. Dad's finally free.

———

At home, I take out my journal from two years ago. I left the last page blank for today.

Dear Dad,

You'll be glad to know that the legislation for medial assistance in dying finally passed in June. Eligible Canadian adults can now request MAID. We held off scattering your ashes until after it became law, the way you asked. We took you out to Lenny's camp in the woods today. Mom was with me. Being able to honour your wishes feels like a small win.

I know how important the legislation was to you. You didn't want it passed only for yourself. You said all terminally ill people should have the right to end their own suffering if they choose. You were right about the bill eventually becoming law. You had more faith than a lot of us. I just wish it would have become law while you were here to see it. The life expectancy of someone diagnosed with ALS is three to five years, and we had you with us for almost five. None of it was easy, but we stuck together the way families do. We learned to lean on each other.

With this final entry, there comes a sense of closure. I've filled three more notebooks since this first one. The other day, I remembered the opinion piece I wrote for the school blog a few years back, "Still a Great Dad." It got me thinking that I could write an article to help people understand what caregivers go through when someone in the family has an incurable illness. There are probably magazines out there that would be interested in my perspective as a teen. It may take a while to get my thoughts together. But one day, I will. Dad always said, "Do some good in the world," and I know that would make him proud.

I've been out to visit James and Frankie. Each time I'm there, James ropes me into doing some work for him. Which got me thinking about the program Frankie's a part of. I've written a proposal and submitted it to the local nursing home. I think I can get some teens on board to help out one Saturday a month. Even Noah says he'd be in, at least during the off-season. We'll hang out with the seniors and talk, maybe read a bit or play some cards. Older people have plenty of interesting stories to tell, something I learned from James. I think the idea is going to fly. Mrs. Britton seems keen on hearing more. I have an appointment with her later this month.

Fall tryouts are coming up in a few weeks. I've been practising with Noah and it feels good. Coach is anxious to see what I've got. If I don't make it this time, I can always try out next spring. With all the other things I've got going on, it won't be the end of the world if I don't.

Rosie's ashes sit on my dresser. I place my notebook beside them. I like having her nearby. There's scratching at my bedroom door, a soft whimper. Jumping off the bed, I open the door.

"What's your problem?" Tucker whimpers in my arms. "Time to go outside before you do something that gets us both in trouble, boy." I fasten the leash and he darts toward the front door. We've only had him a week, but he's catching on. For a long time, I didn't think I'd want another dog. Just too painful when something eventually happens. But I'm ready now and it's all good.

Tucker sniffs the grass, then stops for a moment and takes a pee. It a little weird having a new member in the family. I tug on the leash.

"Let's go for a walk, boy." He looks up at me and makes a small yelp.

I straighten back my shoulders, look out at the sidewalk. We're going to be okay, Mom and me.

"Let's go, Tucker," I say and we start walking. From here we'll all move forward. But no matter what lies ahead, we'll never forget what's in the past.

ACKNOWLEDGEMENTS

MY GRATITUDE GOES OUT TO THE TEAM AT NIMBUS Publishing and Vagrant Press for putting your faith in me once again. Much thanks to Whitney Moran for accepting Sam's story for publication and to Claire Bennet for looking after all the important details along the way. I appreciate all that you do.

Once again, I am so grateful to Penelope Jackson for easing me through the edits of this book and for encouraging me to reach far beyond my comfort zone. You were right, it was worth it! Your encouragement and belief in my writing ability keeps me striving to do better.

To Natasha, hockey mom extraordinaire, I am grateful for the information you shared with this hockey novice and for reading the hockey scenes to make sure I got it right.

My gratitude to my siblings, Tina, Wanda, Randy, and Kelly, for standing by me during challenging times. Your support means the world to me. Love you all!

To Melanie, Michelle, Matthew, Brad, Stephanie, and Alicia, my thanks for your valued opinions and for being a welcome distraction when I'm deep into writing and edits. They say laughter is the best medicine and I thank you all for the fun and laughter you bring into my life.

To Rosie, the inspiration behind Sam's beloved dog in the story and a much-loved member of the Best family, may you have many more years to run and play and bark.

To Brian, thank you for being my light as we journey through this life together.

RESOURCES

IF YOU'RE A CAREGIVER
Young Caregivers Association:
      youngcaregivers.ca
Young Caregivers Connect:
      youngcaregiversconnect.ca
      Caregiver Helpline: 1-833-416-2273

IF YOU'RE GRIEVING
Canadian Alliance for Children's Grief:
      grievingchildrencanada.org
Children and Youth Grief Network:
      childrenandyouthgriefnetwork.com
KidsGrief.ca:
      kidsgrief.ca

IF YOU NEED MENTAL HEALTH SUPPORT
Canadian Mental Health Association:
      cmha.ca
Kids Help Phone:
      kidshelpphone.ca
      call 1-800-668-6868 or text 686868
Wellness and Emotional Support for Youth Online:
      wesforyouthonline.ca

ANGELA HAGGERTY

LAURA BEST IS THE AUTHOR OF SIX BOOKS for young people including *Cammie Takes Flight*, which was nominated for the 2018 Silver Birch Award. Her work has appeared in literary magazines and anthologies across Canada. Her first novel for adults, *Good Mothers Don't*, was published in 2020 and was nominated for The Jim Connors Dartmouth Book Award. She lives in East Dalhousie, Nova Scotia, with her husband, Brian. Visit her at lauraabest.wordpress.com.